I0534800

Typewriter Pub, an imprint of Blvnp Incorporated
A Nevada Corporation
1887 Whitney Mesa DR #2002
Henderson, NV 89014
www.typewriterpub.com/info@typewriterpub.com

ISBN: 978-1-68030-994-2

Praise for The Hunting Game

The book is different from other werewolf romances, breaking taboo about being fated to the one given by god, 'soulmate'. Leila Vy brings romance, betrayal, adventure and great sex under one book. The characters will make you fall in love.
-Anushka Nayan, Goodreads

When I read the book the first time, it blew my mind away. When I read it the second time, it had the same effect on me. The characters are realistic and yet unimaginable. They haunt your dreams until you read the next chapter or the next book. For me, this is a real life fairy-tale.
-Suhani Ritu Swaytank

This book is amazing. It has drama, love, suspense, and much more…
-Zareth Perez

THE HUNTING GAME

LEILA VY

type writer pub

*I want to dedicate this book to my loving husband
who has supported and stuck by my side no matter what life throws at us.
His words of encouragement and motivation for me to continue
what I am most compassionate about, made me a better person today.*

*I know life can be hectic, especially with five children and our busy lives
but what matters in the end is that we made it.*

CHAPTER 1

PATIENCE

There are three important stages in a werewolf's life—the first shift, the first hunt, and meeting his mate for the first time. Meeting one's mate was supposed to be the most wonderful thing in the world. When he first saw me, I expected him to welcome me into his arms lovingly. I expected his words of love to be spoken to me, but I never expected him to reject me.

The sky was of a pale gray. The wind blew hard, whipping the branches on the trees in a fury as I looked at my mate, who stood on the stage in the middle of the field with his arms wrapped around his *chosen*. The pain in my chest and the tug in my bond was too much to bear, and tears were brimming in my eyes. I inhaled sharply to stop the agony as I saw my mate leaning in to kiss his chosen on the cheek. My wolf howled sorrowfully inside of me, and I couldn't help but let us both dwell in each other's affliction.

When he pulled back, his dark blue eyes sought mine. His gaze remained still, and I stupidly pleaded with my eyes to choose me. He turned his gaze away from me, and all I wanted to do was run away from the scene in front of me, but I stood and looked at them.

He looked handsome with his blond hair blowing in the wind. His boyish smile was shining as he stood in front of his pack. My wolf whined and begged me to take what was given to us by the

Moon Goddess herself, but I couldn't. The woman standing next to him was my older sister—his girlfriend—the one he had always loved.

How cruel was fate to pair me up with my sister's boyfriend? The one male I couldn't have. At this moment, I hated fate. When my sister turned to me, I put on a fake smile and clapped my hands. The tears on my face were mistaken for happiness. After looking at me, she turned back to her would-be pack and gave them a good luna smile.

My parents knew about it, but I begged them not to tell anyone who my mate was. They stood next to me and looked at what should have made them happy but were torn at the same time because their other daughter was in turmoil. My sister only knew a made-up name of who my pretense mate was. She didn't know the truth. I squeezed my mother's hand, and she turned to look at me with her loving chocolate eyes.

"Are you okay, darling?" she asked quietly.

"I'm okay, Mom," I whispered.

She lifted her other hand to my cheek to wipe away my tears before turning to look at her other daughter.

After giving his speech to introduce their official luna, my mate turned towards my sister and pulled her into his arms. He pulled back her hair to expose her neck. His canine flashed for everybody to see, and my heart stopped beating. My breathing became labored, and I squeezed my mom's hand in a grip, which I knew must be painful for her.

He was going to mark her. Werewolves mark their mates once they find them. It's a sign of possession and belongingness. It connects the two wolf souls and completes them and keeps them sane. This mark is a symbol of love and nothing more. Stories had been passed that marking helps the two mates speak to each other through their minds but the truth is, it is simply a mark that puts a sense of attachment. It connects both like nothing else in the world. Now, he was going to give it to my sister.

I'm okay.

I'm okay.

I'm okay.

I chanted in my head as I kept looking straight ahead. I felt a searing pain shot through my heart the moment my mate bit into my sister, A and my body shook. I let out a strangled scream and clutched at my mom's arm. "Harold!" she shouted. My dad came to my side immediately and picked me up while I began to feel the world shifting around me. A whimper escaped my lips as the ache in my chest magnified.

"Mom . . ." I roughly whispered with tears running down my cheeks. "Dad . . . "

"It's okay, honey. Breathe. Breathe for me," my dad soothingly urged me.

"It hurts," I cried. "Why does it hurt so much?"

"It will be over soon," my mom's voice broke into my haze of pain.

I felt myself being placed on a soft bed of pillows. The burning sensation from my heart surged into my neck. I felt like a porcupine who had all her spikes removed and left with no barriers to protect her from any pain. The sharpness of the pain was killing me slowly. My eyes fluttered closed, and I felt a hot liquid run down my mouth to the back of my throat.

"Swallow," my mom said, and I gulped it down. "Good girl."

It didn't take me long but soon after, I allowed darkness to take over and fell asleep. The fiery pain in me was slowly dimming.

When I woke up, I heard whispers outside my bedroom. There was a harsh voice who demanded obedience as he spoke. My father's voice growled out an angry "no" to the other person, but his harsh bark back at my father silenced my father's disobedience.

The door to my bedroom swung open and a beautiful, comforting smell swept into the room. My heart began to beat faster; my chest rose and fell rapidly. I refused to open my eyes to meet the person I did not want to see.

"I know you are awake," he said huskily. My eyes fluttered open to meet his, and I felt the strong tug at my heart again.

"What are you doing here?" I asked.

"I came to see if you are okay," he replied as he sat down on the bed. "I am sorry, Patience. I am sorry fate made us mates, but I cannot have you as my mate. I love your sister."

I gulped the lump in my throat and nodded. "I told you I understood. Please leave, Alpha. I do not want to see you. It would only make things difficult on my wolf and me."

"Patience . . . " He exhaled slowly. is hand moved to touch my cheek. Sparks flew and my body responded immediately. I turned to look at him as my body couldn't resist him.

"Please," I whispered gruffly. "Please leave me alone."

He sighed, and I felt the bed lift as he stood up and walked to the door. He stopped before opening it and turned to look at me and walked out. My heart felt like it was being ripped in two. I felt like I died and my heart was burning in fire oil.

My dad came walking into the room and sat in the same spot where my mate sat in. He sighed and looked at me sadly.

"I couldn't stop him. I am sorry, Patience. I tried."

"I know, dad," I replied.

I inhaled deeply. I made my decision after talking to him and seeing what happened today. I have decided not to wallow like a pathetic reject. I wanted a second chance. I wanted someone who cared for me. I turned to my dad with a look of determination on my face.

"Dad, I want to go to the yearly hunting game next week."

It was my last attempt for happiness. If going to the games would give me a chance to leave the pack and hopefully find someone for me, I would go. Nothing was going to stop me.

CHAPTER 2

PATIENCE

When I told my father I would be joining the games, he was hesitant at first but he knew there was no hope for me in my pack. He went to my mate—the alpha—to inform him of my decisions.

My mate's natural instinct was to protect what was his. His human side did not want me, but his wolf desired me and knew who I was. My first and second requests were denied immediately.

I went up to him personally for my third request.

"Alpha, I need to speak with you," I spoke as I chased after him down a dirt trail that led onto the training fields.

"What is it, Patience?" he asked. His blond hair was flying all over in the wind but he still looked handsome.

"Can you at least stop so I can speak with you directly?" I growled out as I picked up speed to get closer to him.

"Just say what you need to say."

"Fine. I am joining the hunting game this year." He stopped abruptly, and I slammed right into his hard, muscular back.

"Goddess," I mumbled as I took a step back to give us enough space.

"You aren't going." He turned to look at me with angry black eyes. Werewolves', eyes turned from their normal eye color to pitch black when they were angry or expressing desire.

I crossed my arms under my chest. "You can't stop me."

"I can and I will. I am your alpha, and I am telling you it's a 'no'." He growled out.

"Then I rather you not be my alpha. I will leave this pack against your wishes. This will forfeit my right as a pack member, and I understand I will earn myself a rogue title." I spat back heatedly.

A werewolf rogue is a lone wolf with no pack attachment. They are easily targeted and vulnerable to attacks, but they can also become ruthless and uncontrollable. Kyle's shoulders were stiff and his breathing was uneven, trying to contain his dominating wolf.

"Don't test me, Patience." He gritted out.

"I am not here to ask you for permission. I am here to inform you of my *decision*," I responded and spun around to go back up the trail to the pack house. I heard him growl behind me, and I was suddenly lifted and carried to a secluded area. He pushed me against the tree hard and pinned me with his body.

"This is hard on me, Patience. Every atom in my body screams for you," he said through clenched teeth. My eyes were not leaving his dark black ones. "I want you."

My heart fluttered and melted at his words, and I couldn't stop what I felt. Regardless if he was my brother in law, my wolf recognized him as her mate. She was prone to affection towards him.

"But I love your sister." My heart crushed again for the hundredth time.

"Then let me go," I pleaded. "This will benefit us both. You can go on living without me."

His nose trailed from my neck to my jaw and back down to the curve of my neck. He paid no attention to what I was saying.

"You smell amazing. It is a scent that I have come addicted to."

He growled out and I felt his lips on my neck. A whimper escaped me unwillingly. My wolf was clawing to escape to meet her

6

fated mate. Fighting against a powerful force inside of you that you can control was emotionally and physically draining.

"No," I mumbled and gathered enough strength to knee him in the groin. He pulled back immediately in shock before bending over in pain. "Kyle, you are my sister's chosen. You sick bastard! You chose her! From the moment you did, you had lost every right to me."

His head slumped and his shoulders drooped in guilt. I spun on my heels and ran back up the trail and away from him. He didn't come after me.

In the end, he allowed me to join the Hunting game but he was still angry. My parents dropped me off at a neutral territory for all werewolves. Kailyn didn't come along with us as she was needed at the pack house. Instead, she wished me "good luck" before I left home. I loved her because I know she had done everything for me. However, I couldn't tell her the truth why I had to do this. Thankfully, Kyle wasn't there when I left. I knew he would stop me if he saw me leaving, which would make it hard on both of us.

The line to register was long and a little crazy as they asked us with deep and personal questions. They led us to a room where they prepped us on what to do. A part of me thought about it as barbaric, but we are animals and this is what we do.

I was excited but scared. What if no one would want me? If my own mate rejected me, what was to say these males wouldn't discard me too?

"Hi!" a voice came to my side. I turned to see a petite blonde girl looking at me. "My name is Tina."

"Hey," I murmured. "My name is Patience."

"Nervous?" she asked.

I shifted uneasily in my seat. "Yeah. A little."

"You don't have to worry at all. You will be fine. Did you lose a mate, or got rejected?" she asked curiously.

"Rejected," I said quietly. Tina gave me a sympathetic look—one that I have seen too often.

7

"I'm sorry. I lost mine in a battle," she said quietly and I felt sorry for her. She must have suffered just as much. "It is okay though. It is time to move on for both you and me."

I nodded as one of the workers ordered us to stand and walk through a door while handing us a long red cloth.

"Put this on and do not take it off. Put your hand out to hold the shoulder of the one in front of you. Once you exit, you will be led to a clear opening where the game will begin."

CHAPTER 3

PATIENCE

The hunting game was held on a neutral territory by Alpha King. The land was a 100-acre land of woods, rivers, streams, and heavy thick grasses. We stood at the northern border of the territory in a single file line. All females were ordered to stand in a single line with a red cloth over their eyes. There were excited voices and whispers amongst the females, and I could distantly hear the whispers of the males that were a couple of miles away from us.

The wind was harsh and before they could place the cloth over my head, I saw a glimpse of the gloomy dark sky. The wind whipped harshly against our bodies, and a faint sweet woodsy scent trailed my way. I inhaled deeply and felt my uneasiness fade away but it soon disappeared as quickly as it came.

The rules of the hunting games were simple: You must be a rejected wolf, or your mate had died to participate. In our world, the males dominated females; the urgency for a male to find a female was higher than a female needing to find a male. The females were behind a white borderline with their eyes covered with a cloth to avoid them from seeking their own chosen. The male wolves were given a chance to look at their choices before females were released into the woods for the males to chase.

Personally, I hated the rules. It was sexist but it was put in place for a reason. I exhaled slowly as the host announced the first group of males to approach us. I thinkk in this hunting game we had well over 100 females and more than 150 males.

The process took a long time. I felt and smelt every male who walked by and sniffed us out. It was supposed to be a quick sniff and move along kind of deal and it took a while due to the male making sure that the female they have chosen was someone who was capable of bearing children or strong enough to stand next to them.

It wasn't until I smelt that sweet woodsy scent again that my heart started to beat fast. It crawled closer to me, and I brought in my lower lip in between my lips to stop the rising emotion inside of me. My wolf was on alert as she also adored the smell as much as I did. I felt somebody's nose gently trailing from my shoulder to the crook of my neck. A shiver ran down my spine. No one had done this to me except this time, but my body responded with tingles and his smell was intoxicating.

I could feel his power radiating through to me. He was making his presence known to my wolf and me as if marking his territory and learning it carefully. I swallowed hard.

When his nose reached the crook of my neck where my pulse was, a low throaty growl rumbled from his chest trailed up my arm, sending a spark down to my core. No words were spoken. It was just his nose and lips tracing my neck to my jaw. When he reached my ear, he spoke in a low, raspy voice.

"You're mine, *ma cherie.*" His accent was prominent as he spoke huskily. He then nipped my earlobe before licking it gently and pulled back.

I bit my lip so hard that it bled and then I felt his finger on my lips as he pulled it out. He used his thumb to wipe and soothe the pain before he was gone, and the smell of him became distant. Who was this male? He scared me and made me excited at the same time. I felt something I thought I would never feel again—hope. My wolf was hopeful and was reflecting it to me.

10

"You may take off the cloth around your mask." The announcer spoke, and I slowly lifted my hands behind to remove my mask. My eyes adjusted to the light around me and when everything became clearer, my eyes darted up to look at the tall male presenter who was dressed in formal wear for royals. He had a white jacket on with a blue sash wrapped around his shoulders.

"The male has until dawn to catch their chosen female. Females have a thirty-minute head start. On my mark, you will begin to run into the woods. The borders of the territory are marked in red. Make sure you do not cross over." The counting had my heart skipping with anticipation. When the announcer counted to ten, the horn blew, and I burst into a run. A part of me was thrilled at the chase while another part of me was afraid of who would be catching me. All females will not go unmated after this.

When we were closer to the edge of the woods, the females began taking off their clothes before shifting. .I took one glance behind me and saw that the males were also taking off their shirts, revealing their naked bodies slowly one by one. My gut twisted, and I ran faster, shifting in air and landing on my paws. I ran for the thrill and the anticipation.

Loud, ferocious growls were heard from behind us as the males asserted their dominance. I jumped over a log and then walked through a small stream, shaking my fur when I got to the other side. I was far enough from the clear opening. The only sound I could hear were the animals and creatures hiding in the bushes.

I trotted alongside the stream, hoping that the water would at least mask my scent for a while until I hit a clear opening with high grass and saw a little bird flying around. My wolf and I were temporarily distracted, jumping and barking at it playfully and temporarily forgetting the thought of the males behind.

CHAPTER 4

PATIENCE

I hopped around the high grass in an attempt to catch a bird that was toying with me as it flew from one area to another. A growl escaped my lips as I went down on the ground to sneak attack it. When the bird landed on a fallen log on the ground and began chirping, I hid behind the tall grass peeking at it. When it turned its back on me, I launched myself at it, only to make it fly away. I huffed and barked at it in annoyance before trotting away.

I walked a few steps towards it before my ears perked up. Every part of my body was telling me to run. It was then that I heard the sound of paws hitting the ground and quickly catching up. Oh no! I totally forgot about the game. *Goddess, Patience.*

I turned my head slightly to see a brown wolf chasing after me. I quickened my pace and merged out from the tall grass into the woods. I didn't know where I was going but all I knew was that I needed to run. I thought I lost the brown wolf but there was no such luck. It was still trailing after me with a look of determination on his face as it was getting closer to me.

When he was close enough, I heard him growl as he was about to pounce me, and I dodged to the left, surprising him. He fell to the ground before getting up. I stopped and turned to look at him. He looked furious that I tricked him. At that moment, I heard another fierce growl from my left that had my wolf ears flattening in submission. I turned to see a tall black wolf approaching us. His stance erected, his teeth bared, and his ears and tail were high to show his dominance.

Ok, if I said I was afraid of the brown wolf. I was more afraid of this big black wolf. He was huge. His piercing blue eyes were staring at me before turning towards the brown wolf who was trying to fight off the growl command that the big black wolf did.

The brown wolf looked at me indecisively, and the black wolf did not like it. His fierce growl came loud and clear before I saw the black wolf launching at the brown wolf, biting him around his neck. Instinct pulled in, and I whipped around and broke into another run. Whatever they wanted to do, they could do it without me.

I ran not even 100 yards when I was pounced to the ground. My belly hit the ground and my legs went down. I growled my irritation and tried to snap my jaw at who tried to stop me. I thought I heard the wolf behind me with a wolf laugh. I struggled to get away from him, but he clamped his jaw down at the back of my neck like we would do to little pups. My struggles were futile. I huffed and slumped on the ground as he released me enough for me for him to get off a little. I heard faint rustling until I heard him.

"Shift," he commanded, and I found my body responding without my will. I shifted right under him. How did he do this? I had no clue. When I was completely naked in front of him, I curled into a weird fetal position.

My eyes flew open to see a tall male with obsidian hair. His familiar piercing blue eyes were looking at me with clear desires in his eyes. My eyes roamed his body with no shame until I got to where he had his shorts on. He must've put them on when I was laying on the ground. Overall, he was tall with muscular build and dangerous. I took a deep breath.

He went back down until he was hovering over my body. His nose was trailing up my arm to the crook of my neck.

"Mine," he whispered, and that prominent accent broke through my embarrassment. He was that male from earlier.

"Can I at least get a shirt?" I whispered, and my cheeks heated up.

A low rumble developed in his chest, and I knew it all too well that he liked what he was seeing and was expressing it in an animalistic way.

"Say it, *ma cherie*," he whispered huskily. His hand was around my waist, lifting me onto his lap where he continued to nuzzle my neck.

"Say what?" I asked. He chuckled before he nipped at my ear playfully for my forgetfulness.

"Say you're mine," he repeated. His scent wrapped around me, and I found myself nuzzling closer to his body, enjoying this new weird tingling feeling running between our bodies.

"How are you doing this?" I asked. "You were able to make me shift that only my Alpha could do."

I felt him grin against my neck as he said huskily, "It seems your wolf has found herself a new *alpha* and *mate*."

My heart skipped a beat with excitement as I processed the information he just gave me. Was what he said true? Did my wolf switch allegiance without me knowing? In my guts, I could feel it though. The connection I had with this male was undeniably strong; not as strong as with Kyle but close enough.

"What is your name?" he asked.

"Patience," I answered.

"Beautiful name," he said gently then turned my chin towards him with his hands. If I thought his eyes were piercing blue, now up close it looks like I was considering the sky as his irises had hints of cloudy white in it mixed with blue. They were captivating with those white clouds in his irises that seemed to move around slowly like actual clouds.

"You're mine, Patience," he said as he looked at me without leaving mine.

CHAPTER 5

PATIENCE

"You're mine, Patience."

It felt like an out-of-body experience. I couldn't control my own actions, or my responses. It was like he put me under a spell. He wasn't perfect but his imperfection was what made him intriguing and beautiful. The old scar t under his left eye extending to his jaw made him look dangerous. The way his mouth was shaped could make a female fantasize what he could do with it.

His eyes darkened, and he let out a growl as he lifted his nose in the air to inhale. My hormones were releasedas I found him attractive and capable of being my mate. This was one thing I couldn't hide.

"There are many things I would enjoy doing right now to you, but I need to get you back before any other male decides to have you. I need you safe," he said. His voice was a tad lower than earlier.

He lifted us up to standing in little effort and then bent down to grab a dark red shirt to slip over my head, marking me as his and taken.

"Get on my back," he ordered as he walked in front of me, which was also a natural thing. He and his wolf were already wanting to pamper us. I propped my hand on my waist and shook my head.

He growled his impatience as he grabbed my hand and wrapped them around his neck. His hands slipped under my thighs to carry me. I had no choice but to wrap my legs around him.

"So, we are going back to the start line?" I asked.

"Yes," he said simply and burst into a run as we zoomed through the woods at a fast speed. Everything was a blur around us.

"What happened to the other male?" I asked, moving my lips closer to his ear. He turned slightly before turning away.

"I killed him."

My body stiffened at his cold indifference. He tightened his grip around my thighs as if I might just jump off him and run away.

"This is the hunting game, Patience. Males are hunting for their new mates. It is held once a year and because the male population is more in our world, the competition and male testosterone is higher now. Males get ruthless and more feral. Everyone is desperate for a mate. You weren't going to be safe and I eliminated the threat," he said casually.

Well if he put it that way, I guess that would make sense even though it was still very barbaric.

"Plus, that male was going to mark you on spot even if you approve or not," his voice hardened and his eyes glazed over.

He sighed. "*Le cœur a ses raisons que la raison ne connaît point* (The heart has its reasons which reason knows nothing of.) You are mine. I will protect you with all I have."

What did he just say? He was speaking in french so smoothly that even if he was yelling at me, I would think it's beautiful. He sounded wonderful with his low masculine voice. I propped my chin on her shoulder and watched ahead as we broke to the clearing, where many other wolves had made it with their mates with a grin on their faces.

He took me up to the door where we came in from before placing my feet on the ground. He was so tall I couldn't even reach his shoulders. His hand came out smoothly to sweep my hair from my face.

"I will come for you soon," he whispered and then leaned down to kiss me on the lips. His kiss made my toes curl and hand clutching at his shirt as he gently pulled my lower lip into his. When he pulled back, hee looked at me with hooded eyes.

"Wait . . . what is your name?" I asked stupidly.

"Titus. Now go. I will come for you soon, Patience," he ordered, gently turning me around to go back inside the door to my parents who were waiting for me.

I had to go back home. I knew he would come for me after the game. What I forgot to tell him was that my mate was still alive and that he was my alpha. I was sure everything would go fine. Kyle had already marked my sister in front of all of us. He had already picked his chosen.

I met my parents who were waiting outside nervously. I walked over to them in a daze and when they saw my color shirt, their eyes widened.

"You have been claimed," my dad spoke, "by an alpha."

The color of the shirts revealed who you were claimed by: Red, alpha; Blue, beta; Green, gamma. Meanwhile, orange were for low ranks. I nodded and bit my lips nervously.

"What is done is done," my dad said before nodding and ushered me into the car where he handed me a pair of pants to put on.

When we arrived home, Kyle was waiting for us outside the pack house. My sister stood next to him as they waited for us. My parents got out of the car and when I followed suit, he looked at my color shirt immediately. He sniffed the air and then looked back at me. His lips were pursing into a snarl as he smelt the scent of another male on me.

"How did it go?" Kailyn asked.

CHAPTER 6

PATIENCE

"Great," I said, looking only at my sister. Her eyes lit up with happiness, and I felt happy yet angry. She moved to hug me.

"I am so happy for you. You deserve to be happy." I could smell him on her. The inner turmoil happening inside of me was unbearable. My wolf and I wanted to rip out the throat of who took our mate but she was our sister and we couldn't do that to her. I swallowed hard and nodded.

I could feel his eyes on me, and he didn't take them off me for one second. It was burning a hole through the side of my face. That was it. I couldn't take it any longer.

"I'm going to go to my bedroom," I said and pulled back. I made my way upstairs and was about to close the door when it was blocked with a hand. My eyes moved to see who it was.

Kyle.

"What do you want?" I asked, keeping my hands firmly on the door.

"You smell like another male," he growled out.

"So?" I retorted and tried to push the door shut, but he opened it with little effort and walked in, closing the door behind him.

"Don't give me that bullshit attitude." His eyes narrowed to slit, and he moved to grip my arms as he pulled me close to him. "You're mine!"

"I am not yours, you idiot!" I began struggling out of his arms. "I am no longer yours. I have already been claimed!"

His eyes flickered black, and he crushed his mouth onto mine. He pushed me up against my bedroom wall as his hands came up to hold me tightly against him to stop me from moving. He was going crazy. I refused to open my mouth but he bit my lips hard. I let out a yelp but he stuck his tongue inside. My body was humming with a tingling sensation as our destined mate was touching us intimately, but my mind was screaming for him to get off me. This was wrong and with one last hope, I bit onto his tongue.

He let out a curse and pulled back, releasing me. We were both breathing hard. I lifted my hand and slapped him across his face. He turned back to look at me. His eyes were still black as his wolf was on the surface. His canine elongated and he snarled with displeasure. I lifted my hand again to slap him but he grabbed onto it before I could do it. He pinned my hands on top of me as he lowered his face until his eye level was with me.

"You're mine, Patience! He won't be able to touch you," he promised. "I'll make sure you are—"

"Are you fucking insane? You love my sister!" I angrily spat back. "Get off me, or I will scream."

When he didn't let me go, I kneed him in the stomach and ran into my bathroom, locking the door. Once safe, I slid onto the floor and hugged my body. I felt violated. My thoughts flickered back to Titus. God, what was going on? Why was everything so messed up? My heart was beating so fast in my chest that I clutched at it.

WhenI heard him leave, I let out the breath I was holding and stood up to walk to the sink and scrubbed my face to get rid of his scent. When I still felt like his scent was still on me, I hopped into the shower. After I was done, I folded the red shirt and put it away nicely as I slipped on a light blue blouse and some high waisted leggings.

I made my way downstairs to see that everyone was outside talking, but when they saw me coming in, they all shut up. I could feel Kyle looking at me from head to toe, and all I wanted to do was throw a shoe at him so he would stop.

I stood next to my parents, putting my hands behind me. I rocked on my feet back and forth and said, "What's up?"

My dad looked at me and then back at Kyle before glancing back at me.

"Alpha Kyle has some concerns about you leaving the pack. He thinks you should stay a little longer until things settled down first before leaving." My dad said and I could hear the edge in his voice. He was not happy with Kyle.

I turned to look at Kyle's heated and determined eyes that never left me. I pursed my lips and jutted my chin out as I crossed my arms under my chest.

"What needs to be settled, Alpha Kyle?" I asked.

"You need to think things thoroughly first. We can't have you being irrational. If after a month you decide that you still want to go, then we will consider your transfer," he said calmly, but his eyes dared me to defy him. I ran my tongue over my teeth in anger.

"I am not being irrational; I am more than rational. I am damn happy to leave this pack and you will allow my transfer. On a second thought, no. I don't care what you want or not. I am leaving regardless of what you want. You won't be able to stop me," I spat angrily and then spun on my feet to walk away from the group. I wasn't going to stay and listen to his bull crap.

"Patience!" He roared and everyone looked down, but I didn't. My wolf and I no longer considered him as our alpha and we won't obey him. I continued walking away until out of the corner of my eyes, I saw seven muscular men walking up the grass clearing to us.

I turned to look and saw Titus. He was already here. His eyes never left mine, and I turned to face him. His eyes urged me to walk towards him. My body moved at its own accord, and I couldn't control my actions even if I wanted to. Those eyes of his were enchanting like a siren singing a song to lure the men to their doom. A slow, confident smirk appeared on his face as he realized what I was doing and he couldn't be more handsome.

Taking the last few steps closer to my chosen, I lifted my hand up to touch him when Kyle spoke snapping me out of my stupor, "Alpha Titus, what are you doing here in my territory?"

Titus dropped his hand and turned to look at a glowering Kyle who had his eyes on me. I could tell he was trying to fight for control. Titus moved to stand in front of me.

"I am here to take my mate," he said with his voice holding little patience.

*   *   *

KYLE

I was beyond furious. My wolf scratched against my human skin, itching to kill who ever had touched Patience, but I refused to let him out. Kailyn's face appeared in my mind which was the source of energy I needed to push my wolf back.

I still couldn't deny how the scent of another male on Patience made me angrier than ever. I agreed for her to go and I needed her gone. She was right; This was for both of us. I couldn't keep her but I also couldn't let her go.

The frustration that was building up inside of me was killing me. I was constantly on edge and it didn't help that I chased her into her bedroom. I shouldn't have but I did.

I shouldn't have touched her but I did. I felt disgusted. I knew what I was doing was wrong but it felt so right too. A voice in my head was screaming that she was not mine and that I had

21

Kailyn, but the pleasure and electrical sensation I felt when touching Patience told me otherwise.

Kailyn had stuck with me through thick and thin. We were friends when we were pups, and I had always admired her. As we grew older, we became more than friends. The affection I held for her was real. At first, Kailyn didn't want to date me. She knew that sooner or later, we would find our mates.

When we turned of age and were full werewolves, I did find her—Patience. I was elated and immediately wanted to go to her but then I remembered Kailyn. Kailyn didn't find her mate yet. I felt bad for her and didn't want to abandon her. She was everything to me. She was there when I was sick. She was there when I was hurt. Kailyn never abandoned me, and that was when I decided against the bond. I figured my love for Kailyn would overcome my bond with Patience. I ignored Patience and the bond. She tried several times to talk to me but I told her I did not want her. I saw the pain in Patience's eyes. She was broken from my words but I also felt a part of me chip away.

Still, I chose Kailyn. I marked her and made her mine. It was my decision but my wolf was still there. I was still the animal that I was. I needed Patience and I craved her touch.

I stayed away from her as much as possible. I slept with Kailyn one night and took her virginity to prove to myself that I could keep away from Patience; that Patience wasn't anything.

I thought that it would be a powerful moment, but it wasn't. I felt guilt instead of pleasure. I still refused to believe that I needed to give in to this bond—thatI could fight it—I just needed to be stronger.

However, now that I saw that Patience had attracted a male and not just any male but Alpha Titus, it irritated me more than ever. Seeing him appear on my land without my permission and demanding that she was his, had me seeing red.

CHAPTER 7

PATIENCE

I could feel the tension in the air. My parents shifted around uneasily and the power played between the two Alphas was evident. I shifted a little to my right to see what was going on with Kyle and Titus, only to have the warriors from Titus's pack flank me on my sides and back. I was completely enclosed in.

"She is not your mate," Kyle said through clenched teeth. I stood on my tiptoes when I couldn't see what was going on. I huffed and crossed my arms underneath me. I felt Titus's shoulder tensed and his hands curled into fist before he lifted his arms and crossed them in front of his chest.

"She is mine!" Titus growled out. The power radiating off from him was coming in waves.

"She is right here," I mumbled from behind Titus, and I heard snickering next to me. I turned to see that it was one of the warriors with Titus's pack. He had a power aura around him too but not as strong as Titus.

"Release her," Kyle commanded with a deadly low voice. "And leave my territory."

"We will leave your territory with her along with us," Titus replied angrily

"Patience!" Kyle roared my name.

"Ok, how about let's calm down for a second," my dad finally spoke

"She's mine!" Titus roared back and my dad shut up as we felt a dangerous wave of Alpha power radiating through the air.

I placed my hand on Titus's back. I felt his body relaxed immediately. The tingling feeling I had felt with him returned the minute I touched him. Momentarily distracted by the feel of his muscular back, I stared with awe. It was like touching a rock. Suddenly, I heard a growl in front of us.

"Titus, can you please move so I can see?" I asked.

"No," he replied.

"Well, I need to see what is going on," I said.

"No you don't," he replied. "We are leaving."

"You aren't taking her anywhere," Kyle's voice shook, and I knew he was close to losing control.

"Kyle, what is wrong with you? That is my sister and she wants to go with her chosen," Kailyn said. She had no idea what the hell was going on.

"Kailyn, I have my reasons," Kyle angrily spoke out, and I heard Kailyn huffing before she fell silent again.

Titus moved his stance by spreading his feet and uncrossing his arms. His warriors did the same. It was clear they knew they were going to have a tough time leaving.

"Titus, let me talk to my alpha," I said.

"Over my dead body, Patience," Titus muttered.

"Please, Titus. I promise everything will be fine," I said and ran my hand up and down his back to help ease the tension in his body and as a mechanism to allow me to talk to Kyle. After a while, Titus huffed in annoyance and turned towards me.

He placed a hand at the back of my head like what mates often do as a sign of equality and protection. and He placed his forehead against mine.

24

"I'll give you five minutes and if after five minutes I don't see you returning, I will come after you, mate. Five minutes, Patience. I mean it."

I nodded, and he shifted a little to allow me to come out from the tight circle of male bodies. When I came out, Kyle's eyes immediately came to me and looked over me. I walked up to him.

"Can I speak to you alone, Alpha?" I asked. He nodded and turned on his feet to go inside the pack house. I followed behind him until we were in his study with its sound proof walls. He turned around to look at me. His eyes were black with anger and jealousy.

"You will not leave me!" He roared. "I will not lose you!"

I swallowed hard as I felt my heart ripping apart. He was my destiny but he was not being fair. "You made your choice, Kyle. I am not yours any more. It is time we go our separate ways. I deserve my happiness as you have already found yours."

He marched over to me and cupped my left cheek in his hand and the other on my shoulder. He looked down at me. "I can still change this. I can make this work between us. Please, don't leave me."

I looked up into his eyes that have turned back to his color. For a moment, I closed my eyes and relished in the bond of my destined mate before taking it away from my face.

"It's too late," I whispered, and my wolf howled sorrowfully. We both knew we had to leave, and we couldn't stay for him. He had picked his chosen and my sister's heart would be broken if she found out. This had to stay hidden and should never be discovered.

He shook his head. His eyes warped into pain as he watched me in desperation. "I can't lose you, Patience. I thought it was the right thing to do. When I was with your sister, I was okay with having you close by. At least I knew you were safe, but now I feel like my soul is ripping into two. I don't think I can go a day without seeing you."

He swallowed hard, and I watched the apple in his throat bobbed up and down before my eyes flitted back up to his and then he spoke again, "We can still be together."

"You are my brother-in-law now. You mated my sister. You even marked her. I felt it—every single night," I said softly. "This is so wrong on so many levels. It can never work out for us."

I turned to leave but his arms came out and wrapped around me tightly. He pulled me close to his chest as he hid his face in the crook of my neck. I felt wetness on my shoulders and his body shaking.

"Patience . . . " his voice cracked. "Please, give me a month. Don't leave me yet. Give me a month to work something out. I want you. I need you."

CHAPTER 8

PATIENCE

"Kyle, you have to stop," I said softly. "Let me go."

I struggled out of his tight embrace. He held me on tight afraid of letting me go and when I struggled harder, he held on tighter.

"I can't let you go. If I mark you, then the mark from your sister will disappear. You can be mine. Together our bond will be stronger than your sister's and mine," he said desperately. I felt his lips travel from my shoulder to my neck and its trail with a tingling sensation. The bond demanded my body to respond but my human side was sickened by what Kyle was doing.

"Let me go!" I shouted louder and jammed my elbow into his side.

He released me with a grunt. I turned around to glance briefly at him. His eyes were black and he growled as he lunged for me. His canine elongated to take the chance of marking me and make me stay with him. I watched in horror as I saw his desperate attempt.

My body kicked into gear and I ran for the door. I was about to reach it when I felt him behind me. He grabbed my shoulders and yanked me around, pressing me against the door with his body. I let out a cry and curled up my shoulders to ward off his attempt at marking me. He was going crazy. Freaking Alphas! I wanted to punch his guts! He was growling as he tried to bite at my neck but my hunched shoulders stopped him from marking me.

Five minutes, Patience.

I remembered Titus saying. I just needed to hold him off for five minutes.

"Kyle, wait," I shouted. "Please, Kyle."

He paused for a moment. His grip on me was still holding me tightly against the door. I turned slightly to look up at him under my eyelashes.

"Think about what you are doing. Kailyn will be hurt. You said you love her. Fight the bond," I begged and he shook his head.

"I love her but you are mine. You are destined to be my mate for life and you are my luna," he said. "I will be damned if I let anyone near you."

"But you love her!" I shouted. "That should be enough to beat the bond you and I have. If you allow me to leave, then the bond will lessen."

"Over the past four years since I have found out you were mine, I fought it every single second. Why do you think I marked your sister?! I thought it would break the bond but instead, I found myself wanting to be closer to you. I found myself looking at you for approval instead of your sister. I found myself watching you every second as you went around with your life. I can't fight it and as time went by, what was a bond was just not a bond any longer. I love everything about you."

Oh god. No.

"I love the way your hair falls loosely down your back. I love the way your eyes glint with amusement and the corner of your mouth lifts into a lopsided grin when you are happy. When I look at you, my wolf and I are happy.

The thought of never seeing you is enough to drive me crazy. I am not going to lose you. You are mine, and I will do anything I can to have you stand next to me. I don't care what Kailyn thinks. Once she finds her mate, she will feel the same way.

28

She will understand why we need to be together," he continued and I knew he had finally gone mad. My destined mate, ex-alpha, brother-in-law was going crazy. I needed to get away from him. I pushed him away from me, but it only brought us both away from the door and further into the room. I silently prayed in my head for Titus to come.

"Kyle, stop!" I cried out as he tried to open my hunched shoulder to expose my neck. "Titus!"

As if Titus heard me calling for him, he came bursting through the door. His piercing blue eyes saw what was happening and instantly turned black with rage. Kyle released me and turned towards Titus. I flew back to the ground and crawled away from them.

"She's mine!" Kyle growled out as he threw a punch at Titus. Titus roared and punched Kyle in the stomach. "You can't have her."

"No, she's mine!" Titus roared back and threw a punch at Kyle's nose and the sound of bone cracking sounded in the air.

Titus looked dangerous earlier. Well now, he looked lethal. His stance was fatally elegant and the way he was throwing his punches were precise and effective. He was deadly and he was furious with Kyle. The warriors from Titus's pack came into the room. Three of them pulled Titus away from Kyle. The other four moved to flank me from all sides.

Titus was still struggling and growling but wanted to go back to Kyle.

"Crap! We can't calm him down. Damn temperamental alphas!" a warrior muttered. I glanced from Titus to him before looking back at Titus. My feet immediately moved, and I walked over to a struggling Titus that they were pinning onto the ground. My hand shot out to touch his face and his eyes flickered back and forth between black.

"Titus, calm your wolf," I demanded and his eyes snapped to mine.

29

"He tried marking you!" New fury flashed through his eyes and he struggled harder. "I'm going to kill him."

Kyle stood up clutching at his nose. His eyes moved from Titus to me. Titus saw that action and he growled louder.

"Look at her again, mutt. I'll kill you faster than you can blink." Titus snarled and tried to get his hand to be freed.

I turned to Kyle. "I am leaving. We made our choices. You have to let me go."

He looked torn. His eyes pleaded for me to stay. His stance told me he would fight for me until his last breath if I chose him. I could feel it from him even when he did not speak the words out loud. Finally, after looking at me, he turned away with his looking at the wall.

"Leave," he said quietly. His voice was broken, and I saw him swallow hard before walking past us.

I stood up and with the other warriors holding on to their alpha, we walked out of the office down the narrow hallway and the steps to the front door. Titus was still unhappy because he wanted blood, but he couldn't.

When I made it outside, my family stood waiting for me. I hugged them and said my goodbyes. It hurts to say "goodbye" but it was for our own good that I did. This was no longer my home.

When we reached the edge of territory, Titus was finally released and he rubbed his body as he barked out orders to his warriors, "*Nous devons vite bouger et partir. Nous ne sommes pas voulut sur ce territoire et nous n'avons pas assez d'hommes* (We need to move quick and leave. We are on unwanted territory and we do not have enough bodies)."

He growled angrily and ran a hand through his hair in an angry manner. He muttered in french under his breath before he spoke again, "*Si seulement Je pouvez arracher la gorge de ce bâtard* (If only I could rip that bastard's throat)."

30

His warriors chuckled as they began to sprint ahead. Titus grabbed my wrist gently and pulled me behind him as he lifted me up to carry meand broke into a speedy run.

"I'm need to learn French," I muttered.

CHAPTER 9

PATIENCE

The warriors in Kyle's pack were physically fit but as I stared at the back of Titus's warriors, Kyle's warriors seemed smaller in comparison. My eyes went from one male to the other as I rested behind Titus's back. We zoomed through the woods heading to neutral territory.

"Can you stop ogling my warriors?" Titus growled angrily. My lips pursed into a thin line. Did he have eyes behind his head that I was not aware of? How did he know I was looking at them?

"If you don't want me to look at them, which I might add pretty much hard because they are in front of us, where should I look?" I asked. He cursed under his breath before barking out in French again. His warriors immediately rushed behind us.

When I only had a bunch of trees in front of me, I turned to look af the next best thing—Titus.

"How long are we going to run for?" I asked as I watched his soft silky black hair flowing back as he ran.

"We are almost to our vehicles. From there, we will travel to a human territory and take a plane back to Paris," he said.

"Is your hair naturally black?" I blurted out as I watched the way his face twitch to almost a smile before it was quickly gone again.

"Yes," he said.

"It's beautiful," I replied.

"Mate, it is anything but beautiful. I am not a beautiful male," he said with a frown on his perfectly sculpted face.

"Can you put me down so I can run with you guys?" I asked.

"No."

"Bu—"

"No."

"Wh—"

"I said no," he said heatedly and the muscle in his cheek ticked. Angry and temperamental alphas. I huffed and turned to look back out at the scenery in front of me. If he didn't want to listen, we could remain silent all the way. I just wanted to get to know him better.

There was no denying. The moment Titus touched me at the game, there was a strange bond between us. It was as if he was my mate. When Kyle touched me, it left a cool tingling sensation after but when Titus touched me, it was like a burning trail of heat. This was definitely different and something I couldn't figure out on my own.

After staring and counting how many trees we have passed, I fell asleep. It was like counting sheep.

When I woke up, I was on a soft bed. I stood up and felt a little unbalanced before walking to the door and sliding it opened. The minute I stepped out, everyone's eyes flew to me.

I felt intimidated under their heated gaze, but I held my chin high and walked toward one of the empty seats across from Titus. I thought I was handling everything well until I tripped on an object and went tumbling right into Titus's lap.

He let out a growl and everyone turned away. I was pretty sure I was blushing beet red by now.

"I am so sorry," I said, trying to get off from his lap.

"Remove your hand, Patience," he said. His voice was deeper than normal. I glanced down and saw just exactly where they were. The sudden thick, large hardness I felt underneath had my face on fire. My hands pulled away immediately.

"Oh god." I covered my face with my hands. I heard him chuckle and I couldn't take it anymore. I turned around on my feet and walked back into the cabin I had originally emerged from.

When I was safely inside behind the closed sliding door, I fell onto the bed and buried my face into my blanket.

"Stupid, stupid, stupid," I muttered quietly as I pounded the bed.

"What are you doing?" Titus asked, amused. I whipped around to see him staring at me and his lips twitching. Goddess! Even with him fighting off a smile, he was gorgeous. This man was sinfully created to tempt me.

"Nothing," I said and stood up to meet him head on. What was done was done. I had to face my embarrassment.

He smirked and his blue eyes stared right into mine as if he was seeking the truth from me, or making me blush again. Either way, I was not bending.

His eyes sparkled with laughter and he looked at me as if he could see me completely naked in front of him.

"I am sorry that I-I touch your thingy," I stuttered out and mentally kicked myself for sounding not confident.

"Thingie?" He arched an eyebrow as he moved so he was standing only a hair's breadth away from me, forcing me to face the heat of his body and electrical current vibrating in pleasure between our bodies. I swallowed the embarrassing lump in my throat as I looked up at him.

"Yes your thing. Your guy thing," I said and his lips turned up into a devious smirk as he leaned down so his lips were barely touching mine.

"I don't understand, mate. What guy thingie?" He prodded further. I huffed and ran my tongue over my teeth in annoyance. His eyes dropped to my lips as I did so.

His sweet scent wrapped around me, and I was feeling a little light headed.

"Interesting. Care to elaborate, *ma cherie?*" he teased further.

"Oh for moon goddess sake, your cock," I spitted out and his eyes lit up with laughter as he threw his head back and laughed. I pouted and moved to step away from him, but he wrapped his arms around me. I felt his chest rumbling as he laughed. He hid his face in the crook of my neck and I instantly leaned into his body.

When he was done laughing, he turned me around with his arms still wrapped around me still.

"It is completely fine, Patience. *Je suis tout à toi* (I am all yours). You can touch me all you want," he whispered huskily until his lips came down on mine.

CHAPTER 10

PATIENCE

When Titus pulled back from the kiss, I looked into his stormy blue eyes that were staring down at me intensely. His eyes were roaming my face as if he was memorizing everything to heart. His hand came up to cup both of my cheeks and pulled me closer so that our noses were touching.

"You are so beautiful, Patience," he whispered huskily. His scent, his touch, and his words had my stomach all filled with crazy butterflies and made my knees feel weak.

"You are too," I whispered and the corner of his mouth lifted into a smirk.

"Alpha," A voice and a knock came from the other side of the door. We both turned to look at it before I stepped back from his embrace, only for him to pull me back into his arms.

"What is it?" he asked, still looking down at me.

"We are landing in ten minutes," he informed us. Titus answered him back and then wrapped his arms around my shoulders.

"Let's get you seated," he said and walked me out the door into the seat next to him where he made sure to strap in my belt.

I looked at the group of warriors and when Titus saw me watching them, he spoke pointing the one to the right. "This is Gamma Noor, Aaron, Richie, Frank, Gerald, and Tom. My beta is not with me. He is at home watching the pack when we left for the game."

"Everyone will be excited," Noor spoke as he looked at me with amusement.

"Why?" I asked.

"We finally got ourselves a luna," he said excitedly.

That reminded me that I still haven't found out what happened to Titus's mate. The thought of it brought a sickening jealous feeling in the pit of my stomach.

"It is gratifying to meet our luna first before everyone else," Frank, who looked a tad older than everyone, spoke next.

"Every year, he goes to the hunting game and comes back empty-handed." Tom, who had blond hair with what seemed like a broken nose as it looked crooked, gave me the cutest grin. I couldn't help but smile back. He was much younger than everyone else. Titus saw my attention on Tom a little longer than needed so he effectively threw a glare at Tom who turned away.

I leaned into Titus as I whispered low, "Will you stop being so possessive?"

He pulled back and spoke loudly, "You aren't marked. That means any male can still mark you. It is natural for my wolf to feel possessive over you. I can't stop—"

"Ok," I quickly butt in as I felt heat crawl up on my cheeks. He placed two fingers under my chin and pulled me towards him again.

"I will try not to be possessive but it is in my nature. I am an alpha, and I am extremely protective of my mate and what is mine," he said and everyone nodded their response from the corner of their eyes as they approved their alpha's admission.

"We are also very protective of you. You are our luna. We will protect you with our life," Noor confirmed.

I felt like I was learning something new for the first time regarding mates. Was this why Kyle was feeling the need to keep me close to him? Thinking about him again and what had happened made me feel upset. Strangely, now that I am away from Kyle, the bond that I felt from him seemed weaker than normal. I could still feel him but not as much anymore.

It seemed my bond with Titus had become stronger like a glowing string that was brighter than the other. I couldn't explain it but I felt the pull more towards Titus, now that I was away from Kyle.

Moments later, I felt the plane prepare for landing. When it landed and the engine was shut off, we unbuckled and stood up to go to the side door which it flew open and stems led down to the ground were extended.

"Welcome to Paris, mate," Titus murmured as he walked up to my side, dipping his head low to my ear.

"Does the whole pack live in Paris?" I asked, clearly confused. Usually, werewolves were hidden from the human eyes and society. We liked to keep to ourselves. He shook his head.

"We don't live in Paris. Our pack resides in the countryside a few hours from here," he said, and I nodded my head in response.

He spoke to some people in french, and Noor moved to join in on the conversation before Titus nodded his head and moved towards me where he placed a hand on my back and led me to the car where the other warriors were waiting.

I settled into the side of the car as Titus sat next to me. Noor hopped into the passenger seat as Frank was the driver. Tom sat next to Titus and Gerald next to Tom. We were so close to each other because these men were giants. I felt squished. I moved myself closer to the window only to have Titus shifted closer to me. I looked up at him and although he wasn't looking down at me, his smirk told me exactly what he was doing.

Titus was imprinting on me as much as he could with his thighs touching every inch of my thigh and his hip touching every inch of my hip all the way up to my shoulders. I sighed and turned to look out the window.

As we passed by the city, my eyes looked around at how beautiful Paris is. In the pictures and books, it was a mirror of it all. Everything was beautiful. I couldn't stop looking, and when I saw the Eiffel tower for a brief moment, I turned around and touched Titus's hand.

"Look! It's beautiful!" I said breathlessly. "I want to see it all day."

He smiled at me spoke, "If you would like, I can take you back here after meeting the pack and performing our mating ceremony."

My smile slipped from my face. I had to meet his pack. What if they won't like me? What if they would see me as not a fitting luna?

His eyebrows furrowed with concerns, "What's wrong?"

"What if they don't like me?" I asked.

He gave me a gentle smile. "You don't have to worry at all. They will like you."

Noor was looking up at the rearview mirror with worry and uncertainty. Why did Noor's expression dictate what Titus just said? I felt a knot form in my stomach as I gave Titus an uneasy smile.

CHAPTER 11

PATIENCE

We drove for several hours until we reached a hidden gravel road where we turned. I turned to look as we entered deeper into the woods. My wolf eyes caught movements and blurs of wolf forms zipping through the trees. Curiously, I looked a little closer and around that blur body to see more of them running through the forest.

"Patrols," Titus whispered next to me.

"They don't know that it is us?" I asked.

"Yes they do. A few of them are following us back while the other watched the border," he replied. I nodded in understanding and watched the bodies zip quickly through the trees.

It took us a while before we reached a clearing and a huge home built with only wood but beautifully built. Titus got out of the vehicle first and I followed quietly behind him. The pack began walking out of the pack house when they saw us coming. Out of the crowd ,a tall black man came walking out with a smile on his face as he looked at Titus.

"Alpha," he said.

"How was everything while I was gone?" Titus asked. I stood behind him staring at his back.

"Not much had happened while you were gone. The border patrols didn't report back any lurking of rogues at the edge of our territory," the man said. I stepped out slightly from behind Titus. His eyes darted to me immediately with surprise clear on his face.

"Who is that?" he asked, pointing at me. Titus, as if he just remembered I was behind him, turned around to place an arm protectively around my shoulders.

"This is Patience. She is my chosen," he announced loud enough for everyone. "Patience this is Christian, my beta."

Christian's eyes grew in surprise as he looked at me carefully before he gave me a smile. "This is a little unbelievable. Sorry for my reaction. I never thought that Titus would finally pick a chosen. You come as a surprise, I think, to us all."

"I hope it is a good surprise not a bad one," I replied back.

He chuckled. "Oh it is a good surprise. It is nice to meet you, Luna."

Out of the corner of my eyes, I saw a red-headed woman staring at us with pain in her eyes. I tilted my head slightly and thought that maybe she was upset with Christian or she was Christian's mate. Titus and Christian saw my momentary distraction and turned to see the red head. When she caught us looking at her, she turned around and disappeared into the crowd.

"Who is that?" I asked.

"That is—" Christian said but Titus cut him off.

"That is nobody you should concern yourself with," he said, and I frowned even more.

"But if she is a pack member, I should be concerned. She—" I said, but was interrupted when he threw me a death glare. I pursed my lips in anger and turned away from him. I didn't want to argue with him in front of the pack. I was going to let this go *for now*.

He sighed, and I saw him run his hand through his thick black hair before he turned to Noor. "Can you take Patience up to my room? I have to speak with Christian."

I curled my hand into a fist to contain my raging anger that was boiling inside of me quickly. Why was he acting this way? We are mates. He should be excited to introduce me to everyone. Shouldn't there be any celebration tonight? Instead, he asked Noor to take me upstairs.

"Is Noor my mate then?" I gritted out.

He turned to me and his eyes turned black. I didn't step down. I didn't know where this newfound confidence came from, but I moved to grab Noor's arm and practically dragged him up to the pack house. We made it inside the house and up the steps before I turned to him looking a little uncertain.

He chuckled when he saw my expression. "You have no clue where to go, do you?"

"No," I murmured.

"Patience!" Titus roared from behind me. I turned slightly to see him coming into the pack house. I grabbed Noor's arm and ran as fast as I could up the steps only for him to run up after me. In one swift movement, he removed Noor from my grip and sent him flying down a couple of steps until he straightened himself. I turned around to glare at him as I gritted my teeth.

"What?" I asked. "I was only doing what you asked."

His eyes were dark as the night when he looked at me. His chest was rising up and down trying to fight for control.

"Don't," he simply said. I sighed and moved my hand to touch his chest. The heated tingles vibrated immediately through us, and Titus closed his eyes. His breathing returned to normal. He opened his eyes in its normal icy blue color.

"Better?" I asked, but he only continued to stare at me. "Now that you have calmed down, I am going to take Noor upstairs to our bedroom as you asked."

His eyes flashed back to black. I saw the clench of his jaw and the rigidness of his shoulders. I sighed. Why was he mad now?

"I'll take you to our bedroom," he said slowly as he grabbed a hold of my wrist and pulled us up the stairs. I turned to look at Noor who was shaking his head with a grin on his face looking at us.

We took several steps climbing up the stairs until we made it to the floor that only had one door. He walked me to it and opened it. When we walked inside, it was beautiful and huge. The bedroom, of course, had big walls and a king size bed. A TV set was to the right of the bedroom with a couch and a small beautiful carved fireplace to the left.

I felt Titus behind me and placed his hand on my shoulders. His face moved to the crook of my neck where my pulse beat as he placed a soft kiss on that spot, and I couldn't help the tremble running through my body in response. I could feel his soft lips trailing up the side of my neck, and I tilted my head to give him better access.

"Patience," he said, and I couldn't help but love the way he says it in his french accent. "How about if you try mine, mate."

I bit my lip and noticed that my eyelids had droop on their own, unable to stop the feeling inside of me. It was like he had placed me under a drug and numbed my mind. He turned me around and his hand trailed from my arm up to my cheek where he cupped it.

"Look at me," he demanded softly. Myeyes fluttered open to look up at him. How could anything icy blue look so heated? My chest was rising fast, and my heart rate was skyrocketing as I silently begged for him to kiss me. As if he knew what I wanted, his lips descended down on mine where he lightly sucked on my lower lip. It was heaven.

When he pulled back enough for me to see his eyes, I could still feel his breath on my lips, "There is just something about you, Patience. It pulls me like nothing I have felt before," he spoke.

I know . . . I know exactly what he meant because it was exactly how I felt with him too. So addictive . . . and . . . beautiful.

CHAPTER 12

PATIENCE

Titus left with a promise that he would return as soon as he finished speaking with Christian. I took the opportunity to glance around his room and sniff his pillows. Yes, I sniffed his pillows. I just wanted to make sure I didn't have to claw any female's eyes out. When I only found his scent, I was satisfied. A faint knocking on the door caught my attention, and I walked over to open it.

A young female who looked and smelt like she recently shifted walked in with a tray of food. My stomach grumbled at the smell of roasted beef soup, and I followed her to the sofa as she sat it down on the coffee table.

"Thank you," I whispered. She looked up at me with surprise in her eyes, and I frowned. Did I say something wrong?

"Y-You're welcome," she said and gave me a smile.

I looked at her warily as she retreated out of the bedroom and closed the door behind her. I sat down on the sofa and picked up the bowl of soup. The smell made my mouth filled with saliva. Without a second to waste, I picked up the spoon and sipped the liquid. The salty beef-and veggie taste hit my tongue like fireworks. I didn't realize how hungry I was until I licked the bowl clean. I was actually really sad when I realized it was all gone.

I didn't know how long it had been but it felt like forever waiting for Titus in his bedroom. I was getting bored so I opened the bedroom door and peeked out. When no one was in sight, I naughtily took one foot out of the bedroom and glanced around again before fully stepping out, then closed the door behind me.

I followed the narrow wood flooring hallway until I reached a pair of stairs leading downstairs. I continued climbing down until it finally took me to the first floor. I followed the smell of beef soup into the kitchen and when I saw no one in sight, I began sniffing around like the crazy wolf that I was. During my search for beef soup, I was momentarily distracted with noises coming from next door.

There were grunting and shouting. Again, my curiosity got the better of me and with beef soup being forgotten, I walked out of the kitchen and down to a small hallway to a glass door where I glanced in and saw a fighting cage. This must be where the pack warrior trained.

This group of warriors were fierce. It was a mixture of female and male together who fought efficiently and quickly. Their movements were so swift they wouldn't be picked up by a human eye.

I placed my hand on the windows, and my nose pressed against the glass. I was awed at how well they fought. When I was in my old pack, Kyle also trained females to become warriors. My father was also a warrior hence, leading Kailyn and I to be trained as well. When it came to the initiation day where we shifted and got chosen to become warriors, Kailyn was chosen to become luna, and even though that day Kyle knew who I was to him, he gave me the warrior position.

Regardless, even if he did choose me to be a mate or not, I loved the training and the aggression. I enjoyed the thrill of competition as well as playing and getting into fights.

"What are you doing?" A female voice asked from behind me. When I turned around to look at her, she quirked an eyebrow at me in question but I gave her a brilliant smile.

46

"This is amazing," I said. Her eyes softened a little bit before she crossed her toned arms. The symbol tattooed on her shoulder indicated that she was a warrior.

"It is. I saw you this morning. You are going to be our luna," she said.

"I am Titus's Chosen," I confirmed her observation and she smirked, glancing up and down disrespectfully.

"If you are going to be our luna, then you have to be strong. Do you even know how to fight?" The flare of anger inside of me pushed my wolf forward and a growl escaped my lips. Her eyes twinkled with amusement. "Well, Luna, will you take me up on a challenge?"

She opened the door and walked in. Everyone turned towards her and she put two fingers between her lips as she whistled now catching the two warriors in the cage. They both broke apart to look at her.

"What's going on, Yenis?" One of the warriors asked as he came close to the cage to prop his arm up as he glanced down at her.

"Out, Brian. I am going to do one-on-one with the luna," she said confidently, and I walked in accepting the challenge. I wasn't going to back down. My wolf refused to cower and I agreed completely.

"Are you sure?" he asked after glancing at me.

I nodded. "I'll be fine."

He turned back to Yenis, "Be careful, Yenis. Alpha will be angry if he sees her hurt."

"She will be fine," Yenis said in a bored tone as she waved her hand for them to exit the cage. She walked in with her sports bra and tight shorts. I felt overdressed as I glanced down at my baggy t-shirt and grey sweatpants. Nonetheless, I still walked into the cage. It closed behind me with a click.

Everyone stood around and watched.

47

I felt a mixture of fear and anticipation. My wolf and I were thrilled to fight again but feared we might disappoint them.

I was the first one to move by throwing the first punch. Yenis grabbed my fist and efficiently flipped me over and caused me to fall flat on my back.

"Oh come on. That was too easy," Yenis taunted on top of me. Her legs were on either side of my waist. I grabbed an ankle and pulled her flat on her back.

We both flipped back up to a standing position. She threw the next several punches hoping to catch me off guard but she didn't know that speed was always my strongest point. However, I noticed she was forcing me back against the cage.

When we got too close, I quickly used the cage to my advantage and flipped over behind her. She turned around quickly and grabbed me by the collar of my shirt. I pulled back and the shirt ripped open.

"That's my favorite shirt!" I growled out angrily. That's it. I ripped the rest of it off and threw an uppercut at her but she only dodged it. I took the chance to kick behind her knee, sending her knee buckling to the ground. I wrapped one arm around her neck exposing one side and placed my mouth by her pulse.

Everything stopped.

"I knew you would be good. I saw it in you," Yenis breathlessly said. "You are better than her."

I was breathing just as hard as she was. I released her and looked around. Everyone was looking with interest but my eyes stopped when they met a pair of blue ones.

"Titus," I whispered but I knew he heard and he looked angry but I can almost feel the pride coming from him.

"Everyone out." He roared and everyone was out the door in second. I was about to leave when he spoke.

"Not you, my dear Patience," he said lowly as he stalked into the cage. I felt trapped. He looked like he was going to eat me alive.

"I can explain . . . I did wait for you in our bedroom but I got bored," I said.

He walked up to me and played with a strand of my hair. "So you decided to come down here?"

"I enjoy fighting," I whispered my reason. His closeness was really missed and I found myself wrapping my arms around his waist. His body relaxed.

"Well you did do a really good job. Everyone will be taking about this for days," he said with a chuckle.

CHAPTER 13

PATIENCE

"So, you enjoy fighting?" Titus asked, clearly amused. I pursed my lips at his reaction.

"Yes. Before I left my old pack, Kyle was going to initiate me to become a warrior for that pack. Kailyn and I were both trained together." Titus growled with displeasure.

"I don't like you speaking his name," he muttered. He began circling me as if he was circling his prey within the cage. I watched him cautiously. When he was behind me, I saw his fist shot out from the corner of my eyes. I moved my torso to the side to avoid his attack. I turned to him with a glare.

"What was that for?" I asked angrily.

He chuckled, "Train with me, mate."

I arched an eyebrow. "Are you sure you can handle me, Alpha?"

His eyes darkened at my teasing and I smirked. Before I knew it, he had his arm wrapped around my neck, and my back pressed firmly against his front. His nose and lips trailed my neck like a soft caress.

"There isn't any part of you that I can't handle. I wonder . . . *est-ce que tu es aussi douce que tes yuex* (Are you as sweet as your eyes are?)" he spoke. I felt his mouth on my neck as he sucked on my sensitive spot. My eyes fluttered close as millions of sparks spread from that small contact all the way through my body. My grip on his arm tightened and just when I felt him lift his lips slightly, I flipped him onto his back and quickly moved to straddle his body, my hands were attempting to pin his arms above his head.

"What did you just say?" I asked.

He smirked at me, and his icy blue eyes glinted with mischief. Surprisingly, he flipped us over. Damn, he was quick.

"*Tu es pour moi la plus belle* (You are, for me, the most beautiful, mate. I am drawn to you like a moth to a flame," he whispered huskily. His lips hovering over mine. His eyelids drooped as he lowered his lips. I pushed him off me and flipped myself up.

"All I could understand is 'belle,'" I muttered. He was not being fair.

He chuckled and that slow, cocky smirk came back onto his face. I growled and moved to punch him in the guts just to let out my frustration at his French taunting. He saw it coming and grabbed my wrist twisting it behind my back. His other hand came to wrap around my neck.

"You need to be quicker than that to keep up with me, *ma cherie*," his voice was like a sensual cloudy wave that was filled with intoxicating drugs.

I stomped on his toe and he let out a curse, letting me go. I turned around and shrugged. "I guess I do."

He turned to glare at me and tried to reach for me, but I wasn't going to fall for that again. I quickly dodged his attack and ran out of the cage. I turned around to close it, twisting the lock. His eyes widened in surprise.

"Patience, open the door," he ordered.

I rocked back and forth on my knees with my hands behind my back as I spoke, "Or what?"

Suddenly, I regret locking my mate and alpha in a cage.

"You will see," he whispered and I swallowed hard. It was too late; I was already in trouble. I jutted my chin out and shook my head.

"I guess you will have to stay locked up then, Alpha," I said defiantly.

"You really going to lock me up here?" he asked, surprised and clearly amused.

I lifted my wrist and glanced at my nonexistent watch. "Oh, would you look at that? I have to go. I'll see you soon."

I spun on my feet and hurried out the door. I heard Titus call my name and when I didn't return, he shouted louder. Uh oh, he sounded angry. I walked down the hall and bumped into Christian and it sent me flying back a couple of steps. I turned to look at the tall dark-skinned man.

"Luna?" he asked, confused. "What are you doing down here? I thought Alpha came looking for you."

I gave him an awkward smile. "Nope. I didn't see him. I got to go."

I ran past him and back up to the bedroom where I went through his closet and pulled out one of his t-shirts and boxers. I walked into the shower and when I turned to look at the window, I saw a love bite on my neck. The sneaky alpha! He intentionally imprinted me. I touched the love bite and felt a tingling ripple through my body before I took off the rest of my clothes and hopped into the shower.

I took a quick shower and pulled on his t-shirt and his boxer. His shirt was so big it looked like a dress on me as it reached mid-thigh. After brushing my hair and leaving it down to dry, I walked out of the bathroom to see Titus standing in the middle of the room looking furious. Uh oh.

When he started for me, I squealed and darted back into the bathroom where I closed the door and locked it. I ran to the other side of the bathroom and leaned against the wall.

"Open the door, mate," he said.

"No," I said.

"Open it, Patience!" He growled out angrily.

"No," I repeated.

It was quiet for a moment before the door came falling down on the floor, leaving no barriers between us. I let out a squeak and pointed at the door.

"You broke the door."

"I wouldn't have broken it if you would have listened," he said angrily.

"We can talk about this, Titus," I offered and his lips curved into a devilish grin that had my gut clenching. Oh dear, he was flipping gorgeous even when he was furious with me. He walked over to me and hoisted me over his shoulder.

"Titus!" I shouted. He carried me into the bedroom where he sat down on the bed, bringing me down across his lap with his hand on my bum. "No. Remove your hand, Titus."

"No," he simply said. "I said you will be punished. So, you will be."

His hand came out to spank my butt. I let out a squeak and then turned slightly to look at him.

"You didn't just spank me?" I asked with a glare.

He arched an eyebrow and with amusement, he said, "I did."

He spanked me again. This male was unbelievable. I struggled out of his lap and he held me down with his other arm as he spanked me a couple of times. I continued to do it until we both went tumbling down onto the floor. I groaned as he fell on top of me.

"Moon goddess above, you are heavy," I muttered. I heard his chest rumbling before a laugh escaped his lips. When he lifted his head, the way his black hair tumbled over his forehead and how his face lit up had me captivated. I completely forgot what we were doing.

"What am I going to do with you?" he asked after he stopped laughing.

"Well . . . " I started, then he lifted his hand.

"I am afraid to hear your answer," he spoke and I grinned. He was starting to know me well. He pulled back and sat down on his butt as he leaned his back against the bed. I moved to kneel between his legs.

"I'm sorry I locked you up," I said.

He raked his hand through his hair to move the hair tumbling over his forehead back and glanced at me. "You are the first wolf to ever defy me."

"How did you get out?" I asked curiously.

"Christian. He came looking for me after he bumped into you. He said you looked guilty," he answered with a grin. I pouted and he laughed as he pulled me back into his arms. "I love you in my shirt. It has my scent all over you. It eases my wolf protectiveness."

"Titus, who was that woman when we first arrived?" I asked and his body immediately stiffened.

"I don't want to talk about it, Patience," he said.

"Why not? If she is your pack member, then you should be able to talk about it. Is she someone close to you? What are you hiding from me?" I asked the questions that were running through my mind one after another

"I said, I don't want to talk about it," he said. I sighed. He moved to cup my cheek to bring me back to look at him. "I can never say no to you, can I? I'll tell you tonight, I promise."

Satisfied, I nodded and then my stomach grumbled loudly. He laughed and lifted me up. "Let's go eat, mate."

"I'm wearing only your boxers," I muttered quietly.

He glanced down and his eyes went dark again with lust. "You should be fine. My shirt covers your body."

I was more than happy to go with him. We made our way down into the dining area where many pack members were already there eating. When they saw us, they all looked up. Many of them were whispering and looking at us. I leaned into Titus and when he saw that I wanted to speak to him privately, he leaned his ear near my lips. I was thankful that he understood.

"Why are they looking at me that way?" I asked.

He turned to me, "They are talking about you beating Yenis."

I blushed as a few people came up to us to talk to us. Titus exchanged a few words with them and then they turned towards me.

"Hello, Luna," the older female greeted me.

"Hi . . .?" I questioned further.

"Oh, silly me. My name is Caroline. This is my husband, Gregory." She pointed to the male next to her. He gave me a smile as he greeted me.

"It is really nice to meet you two. Can I ask for a favor?" I said a little awkwardly. Titus, Caroline, and Gregory turned to look at me. "Can you not call me 'Luna?' It is too formal and I am not used to that title. We are around friends. Please just call me by my name."

Caroline and Gregory turned to look at Titus who nodded. They turned back to me and nodded their agreement.

"We will call you by what you want us to," they said.

"Please just call me Patience," I said and then turned to everyone whom I knew were listening in on the conversation. "I would be grateful if everyone called me Patience."

Everyone grinned and nodded their acceptance in calling me by my name. Titus placed his hand on my back and took me to the head of the table. Everyone followed behind and seated as we waited for dinner.

Everything seemed to fall right into place, that is, until I happened to bump into the redhead from earlier when I excused myself to use the bathroom.

CHAPTER 14

"Can I speak with you privately?" she asked.

A part of me answered *no* but a part of me was curious as to who she was. I nodded and followed her down the hall to a private area not far from the dining room but far enough to not be heard. She turned around once we reached the end of the hall.

"Do you know who I am? Did *he* tell you who I am?" she asked.

I shook my head. "No."

She sighed and her face looked upset and sad. She began sobbing, and I stood there staring at her not knowing what to do. She hiccupped and then threw her arms around me.

"I love him. I am so sorry. I know you are going to be the luna, and I shouldn't say this to you but I feel like I have to. You have to know who I am," she cried and then wiped her tears.

My soul shriveled a little and I felt something inside of me chipped away. I didn't want to hear what she had to say. I didn't know what I was doing until I shook my head. She looked up at me with confusion, and I cleared my throat.

"Who are you?" I croakily asked, feeling the dryness in my throat.

"My name is Amelia. I am his true mate," she whispered back and my soul died.

"If you are his true mate, then why isn't he mated to you?" I asked. . I was doubtful because I knew the bond between Titus and me was strengthening rapidly and could never be controlled.

"He doesn't want me. He wants someone of his choosing," she whimpered. Her eyes were red from crying.

"Did he reject you?" I asked.

She looked at me and spoke, "Yes."

There must be a reason why. There had to be. No wolf would ever reject their true mate if they were sane but my head flitted back to Kyle. He was sane but he still rejected me and wanted someone else. He wanted Kailyn.

"Why?" I asked.

"He says I am not fit to be a luna. I told him I would try my hardest to be the best mate he could have. He said I was flawed and ugly. I can't stand next to him." She sobbed. My heart was touched but I had a gut feeling that told me to not go hopping around and pointing fingers yet.

"Patience." A strong voice spoke from behind me. I whipped around to see Noor looking at us. His eyes glanced behind me to look at Amelia, and I have never seen such cold eyes from him before. It was scary.

"Noor, what is it?" I asked.

"Alpha sent me to come get you. You were gone too long," he said.

I glanced back at Amelia who looked at me pleadingly. I turned back to Noor who was waiting patiently and with the way his hand tightened into a fist, I was sure he wasn't going to leave here without me. I sighed and turned back to Amelia.

"I am sorry. Let me think this through," I whispered gently and then turned to walk back towards Noor. When I was at his side, he waited until I walked forward before following me. I did not miss the glare he had sent Amelia.

"Why are you looking at her like that?" I asked him.

57

"It is not my position to tell you, Patience," he spoke angrily. "But I tell you this:Stay away from her."

This irked me even more. Why was there so much mystery? It felt like I was walking through a dense fog and would never find my way out. Did what Amelia say have any truth? Was Titus a bad mate? "It's okay if you can't tell me, Noor. I will talk to Alpha," I said. He swiftly nodded.

"I suggest speaking with him sooner than later," he urged and when we emerged in the dining room again,Titus was standing around talking to people. Dinner was over.

He stood out above everybody in this room. I wasn't sure if it was because of the bond we share, but I could pick him out in a room with a hundred people. He was just tall and big. His aura radiated his power. He turned to look at me when he felt my eyes on him and my heart picked up speed. Staring into his eyes, my body moved to stand next to him.

He wrapped an arm around my waist and pulled me close as he leaned down to whisper in my ear, "You were gone for a very long time. I was afraid you were at war with the toilet."

"No," I simply said. My mind was still swirling with Amelia's words as I glanced around the room. My eyes landed on her again. She was staring at us. I broke my eyes away from her and glanced back at Titus. He was looking at me oddly.

There was no denying, I wanted and needed Titus. My wolf couldn't face losing this bond. I didn't know why but it felt like it would hurt more if I let him go. As if he noticed the misery I felt, he turned to cup my cheek as he looked into my eyes.

"What is wrong?" he asked. His voice filled with concern.

"Nothing," I said quietly. He shook his head as his hand dropped from my cheek to grab my wrist. He pulled me away from everyone as we walked back up the steps.

When we reached our floor, he opened our bedroom door and when we both entered, he closed it behind me and then he turned to look at me.

"I can feel something is wrong," he said as he approached me. "Tell me."

"Is Amelia your true mate?" I asked and he stiffened. His eyes turned hard and he let out a growl. He was about to turn away from me when I grabbed his elbow. "Tell me, Titus."

"I told you to leave it and I would tell you tonight," he growled angrily.

"It is night and news flash, I have waited long enough! It is time you tell me, Titus. Tell me now," I ordered angrily. His eyes flared up in defiance and his alpha power radiated in a tremendous wave at me. Anyone would have run away the minute his power hit them, but it was me. I met his eyes head on.

"Do not order me around, Patience. Keep in mind who the alpha here is," He gritted out and I ran my tongue over my teeth angrily. The urge to bite was overwhelming. He was pissing me off.

"I understand you are alpha, but who am I to you?" I asked.

"You are my luna and my mate," he growled viciously and his eyes turned black.

My eyes softened and sadness drowned my body as I looked up at him. "That is the thing, Titus. I am not your mate."

He growled again and I saw a flash of his canines. He was getting angrier and his wolf was not happy with my statement. He wanted to make his presence known. He was becoming hostile. He moved to grip my arms tightly as he pulled me up close to him. My lips were inches away from here.

"You are mine," he growled out ferociously. "You will be no one else's but mine. Do you understand?"

I looked up into his eyes that were dark as the night. I wanted to tell him *yes* but Amelia stood in the back of my mind. I shook my head.

He snapped his jaw and I saw his body tremble. "Patience."

"Why did you do it?" I asked. "Why did you reject her?"

"How did you know?" He asked, looking angrier. "Who told you?"

"Tell me. You haven't answered my question," I retorted. He answered my question with one of his own. That wasn't going to pass by me easily. I wanted an answer.

"I don't want to talk about her right now," he snapped as his black eyes stared down at me. His grip on my arms was hurting me now. "You're mine, Patience."

"I'm not yours," I said quietly and he growled loudly. It was the loudest I have heard him. I think the whole house heard him. He yanked me into his arms as he wrapped his thick muscular arms around me. His nose trailed down to my pulse. I remained rigid and still in his arms as soon as I felt the familiar heated sparks go through me. I could see the way his jaw ticked and the way he was growling told me that his wolf was on the surface. He snapped his jaw close to my pulse and then suddenly let me go. I turned to see his canine elongated.

"Stop . . ." I whispered softly. "Please, all I want is to understand."

He covered his mouth with his hand to stop him from biting me. He growled and walked out of the bedroom quickly. I looked at him until he disappeared. I inhaled sharply. I didn't know why I was feeling this way when I was with him. Why was I feeling such a strong bond with him? How could this even be possible when I already had a mate?

Exhausted from all the emotions flying around me, I walked to the balcony in his bedroom and sat on the floor as I watched the moon shine down at us. Silently, I begged for some kind of answer since I wasn't getting any here. I hoped that Moon Goddess herself could tell me what was going on with Titus and me as well as Amelia. I was hopeful that Moon Goddess would take pity and answer my silent prayer.

I leaned my head back and looked at the moon. Slowly, my eyes began fluttering and it didn't take long before sleep took over.

60

I appeared in a room with a beautiful young woman dressed in a red deep v-neck gown. Her hair black as the night trailing down her back as she was concentrating and murmuring under her breath, looking at the r window at the moon.

"Hello?" I said as I approached her. She didn't look up at me. She continued murmuring and when I got closer, I heard what she said.

"One truer than their hearts, one where resistance will be futile, one that is stronger and will not depart. Together, they will become the ultimate mates—bonded by fate for eternity. A bond stronger than all, a bond that has always been tied as one."

I frowned as I moved to stand in front of her. "Hello?"

She was truly beautiful. Her delicate pale skin and heart-shaped face made her look very young, but her golden wolf eyes told me she was wiser than what her image perceived. She turned to me and spoke again.

"One truer than their hearts, one where resistance will be futile, one that is stronger and will not depart. Together, they will become the ultimate mates--bonded by fate for eternity. A bond stronger than all, a bond that has always been tied as one."

"I don't understand," I whispered.

"You need to allow your mind to see it, Patience. See what I have given you." She whispered and it was then that I knew who she was.

CHAPTER 15

I felt something flutter across my face. I pouted and swatted away the offending object that was tickling me. When it was gone, I snuggled closer to what seemed like a pillow. How did I end up with a pillow under me when I was outside on the balcony? I shot up immediately and my forehead hit Titus's chin. I let out a yelp as I held my forehead and glared at him. He was holding his chin when he looked at me.

"What did you do that for?" he asked as he frowned.

"Why did you wake me up?" I retorted.

He broke into a grin. "You were sleeping outside on the balcony. I can't have my mate sleeping out there. I carried you inside. You were murmuring in your sleep. Did you have a bad dream? I crawled into bed with you and as if you knew it was me, you snuggled into my body."

"I did not," I mumbled, feeling heat crawling up my cheeks.

"Oh yes, you did. You snuggled so close to my body I didn't even get to leave. So, I held you all night," he teased, and I groaned as I flipped over away from him to muffle my embarrassment in a pillow.

I heard him chuckling as he leaned over his warm body pressed to my back as he hovered over me. His lips moved to the back of my neck, and I could feel his warm breathing tickling me.

"What did you dream about?" he asked.

I turned slightly to look at him and memories of what I dreamt about flashed through my mind. The Moon Goddess and her riddle were prominent in my mind. I turned completely onto my back and chewed my bottom lip as I tried to remember her riddle.

Titus propped himself on one elbow as he lay down on one side. His muscles flexing as he did that action. Momentarily distracted, I looked at his body and my tongue darted out to lick my dried lips. His messy bed hair look was absolutely sinful. It should be banned and considered illegal. No sexy messy bed hair for hot Alphas.He cleared his throat, and my eyes flickered back up to his eyes which were clearly amused as he saw where exactly I was looking at. I pursed my lips in annoyance.

"Go away," I muttered and flipped back to my side. His arm snaked around my waist and pulled me back into his chest as he nuzzled his face in the crook of my neck.

"You are a difficult female, Patience," he murmured softly as his lips found my skin.

"I thought you were mad at me and intent on hiding things on me," I mumbled finding it harder to be mad at him when he was nuzzling me like that.

He sighed and leaned back a little. "C'mere."

He lifted me like nothing onto his lap. I turned to look at him and all I could think about was how beautiful he looked up close. I wanted to pounce him and eat him up alive. *Kidding!* He does look delicious though. My eyes dropped to his lips before flitting back up to his icy blue eyes.

"Yes?" I asked.

He chuckled, and I guess he was in a better mood today than yesterday. "Amelia is my true mate, and I found it out when she shifted. We were together for a year. She said that she wanted to wait before we did the mating ceremony. So I waited but she lied. She was debating if she wanted her chosen or me as her mate."

He adjusted our position so that he was leaning back against the headboard of the bed, and with me between his legs, his arms wrapped around me protectively.

"I woke up one night in pain. I felt like someone was carving into my skin and slowly taking out my organs without any anesthesia. The next day, I approached her and she smelt like another male and his arousal. I knew what she did," he said and I knew what he meant. I felt the same thing every single night with Kyle and my sister. "You know what she said?"

"What?" I asked quietly as I felt sorrow for him. Nobody deserves to go through that.

"She said she loves me, butbefore spending the rest of her life with me, she wanted to experience what she could have with her chosen," he said as if something bitter was in his mouth.

I turned around to look at him. He gave me a smile and I felt my heart move again in faster beats. He seemed to have that influence on me. His hand came out and touched my cheek, and I closed my eyes, savoring in the heated tingles he gave me.

"Do you feel that?" he asked, and my eyes opened to look at him. When I nodded, he spoke again. "I knew you were mine the minute I smelt you on that field. Your scent was so strong, and my wolf was howling inside of me, demanding to search for the female who had awakened him. When I saw you in that line with that blindfold, I knew it was you. Imagine my delight when I touched you and I felt this—"

His hand moved down to my neck where the heated tangles danced and spread like wildfire.

"I knew you were the one. I knew you were mine and only mine. My wolf wouldn't have it any other way. He has already chosen you as I did too," he whispered. . "*Le coeur a ses raisons que la raison ne connait point.* (The heart has its reasons which reasons know nothing of.)"

"Tell me what that means," I asked and when he said it English, it made me think about what the Moon Goddess had said to me in my dream.

"So, I have gathered that Amelia has spoken to you," he said as his hand dropped from my neck onto his side.

"She—" a knock on the door interrupted me. I turned slightly to look at the door. Titus got up from bed and walked over half-dressed to open the door.

"What is it?" he asked. I heard some muffled voices on the other end and then they spoke in French back and forth. Whatever it was, they didn't want me to know.

I got up and went to the bathroom to brush my teeth, but that familiar burning sensation ran through my body again. I clutched at my heart and my body leaned against the counter to help me. A soft whimper escaped my lips, and I began seeing white as the world began spinning around me. I closed my eyes tightly to try to blink away the blurriness in my vision. Sharp stabbing pain in my guts began, and it felt like needles prickling me all over the places.

I dropped to the ground and curled up into a fetal position as I let the painful tears fall. I haven't fully rejected Kyle yet and the bond with him was still there even though it might not be as strong. I closed my eyes and willed myself to go to a happy place in my mind as it has helped me in the past, but I knew what was coming and this was just the beginning. A few moments later, I felt the needles on my skin dig deeper, and my gut was twisting harder. I let out a cry and used my fist to muffle it as I did not want Titus to see. However, he heard it.

Within a second, he was by my side. He examined my body before he knew what was going on and scooped me up into his chest. He carried me over to the bed where he sat down with me in his lap. He began murmuring soothing words as his hand caressed me all over my body.

65

"You will be fine," he whispered and kissed my forehead. "You haven't spoken the words to him, have you?"

"No," I said through clenched teeth. "Someone was in a hurry."

He chuckled and hugged me closer. "You have to say it. It will help ease the pain."

"I know. I didn't in the past because—" I paused for a moment. "I still had hope."

Titus did not look angry. I looked into his eyes, all I could see was him understanding what I was saying.

"I know it is bad of me. He is my sister's mate now but I thought—I know I am foolish," I said quietly. The nearness of Titus helped ease the pain amazingly. I could only feel tingles of it now.

"You are not foolish. Mates are what we need to survive as werewolves. You were just giving him a chance he didn't deserve. That does not make you foolish," he whispered quietly and then hugged me tighter.

"C-can I call my family?" I asked him. He gave me a soft smile before nodding.

"Get dressed and when you are feeling better, meet me in my office," he said.

The pain has eased completely and I could feel that my wolf and I were a little weak from it, but we should still be fine. When we first felt it, we were in bed for days. It did weaken us so badly I really thought I was going to die.

He sat me down on the bed gently, planting a kiss on my forehead that sent little shivers through my body and then sniffing my lightly before pulling back and headed to the door. I watched him leave me and then got up and got dressed.

I pulled on one of his t-shirts and slipped on one of his athlete shorts that were too big. I pulled on the strings to tighten it up. I really need clothes soon. We left so quickly, I didn't get to pack. I put my hair up into a ponytail and headed to his office for

66

which I have no clue where it was so I wandered around until I bumped into Noor.

"Where are you going, Patience?" he asked.

I awkwardly laughed as I scratched my head, "I am trying to find your alpha's office."

He chuckled and waved his hand for me to go over to him, "Let me do the honor of taking you. You are on the wrong side of the house. His office is actually really close to your bedroom."

We made our way up a few flights of stairs back to our floor and then led me to the end of the hallway where another door was there. He knocked on the door before opening it. Titus was on the phone speaking in French and when he saw us his eyes moved from Noor to me.

"Thank you," I said as I turned to Noor. "You have been very helpful."

"Anytime, Patience," he replied and then turned slightly. "I better get going. If I am late for training, the alpha would eat me for dinner."

I laughed softly at him as he shot Titus a look before smiling and walking out the door. I turned to Titus and he waved at me. I walked over to his side. Immediately, he pulled me into his lap. His nose was burying in my neck as he spoke French every now and then to answer the other man on the other end. I waited patiently for him to finish and when the call took longer, I began touching the stuff on his table.Leaning forward a little I played with his post-it notes as I wrote little notes here and there.

I felt a pinch at my butt, and I squealed a little and I sat up straighter. It was then that I felt that apparent hardness on my back. I turned to look at him and he arched an eyebrow. I moved to get off his lap but his grip around my waist tightened. He placed the phone on mute and leaned in to kiss my neck where my pulse beats.

"You need to stop moving your bottom, my beautiful mate. Otherwise, you and I would be doing something you might not be ready for," he whispered and my stomach fluttered with

67

butterflies. I bit my lip and remained completely frozen in my spot. He chuckled as he un-muted the phone. God, he was really crazy. Crazy alpha mate. Now my body was fully aware of every part of our body that was touching, and I couldn't stop thinking about what exactly we would be doing if I continued to move around in his lap.

CHAPTER 16

I waited patiently until he was done talking before he sat his phone down, then turned my head towards him. I looked at him and licked my lips as they suddenly felt dried and my throat felt parched. His finger moved to trace my lips gently and in its wake, a small heat tingled on my lips.

"So beautiful," he whispered and then his hand snaked through my hair and pulled me down to meet him halfway as his lips molded perfectly over mine.

A sigh escaped my lips as he sucked on my lips several times before slipping his tongue inside. His kisses had me burning on the inside and out. The sensation multiplied, and I felt myself wrapping my arms around him urging him to continue. My toes curled at the overwhelming sensation, and a sound came from the back of my throat.

When he pulled back and started trailing kisses down my jaw line, I tilted my head enough to give him access. He growled his excitement as he saw how willing I was as his mate. He was an intoxicating drug and I loved it. Every time I was around him my mind seemed to be in a numbing state.

"Titus . . ." I whispered. He hummed his response as he sucked on his earlier love bite. "The phone please."

He sighed and dropped his forehead onto my shoulder as he reached for his phone and handed it to me.

"You really know how to kill the mood," he mumbled. I couldn't help the smile that came on my face as I dialed the alpha line. Shortly after, Kailyn picked up.

"Kailyn, this is Patience," I said eagerly. Kailyn squealed on the other end.

"Oh my god, Patience! You called. How are you doing? How is he treating you? Tell me all about it," she said, and I blushed turning the volume down even though I knew either way, Titus would hear everything. His hand was naughtily moving up and down my side.

"I'm doing great. It's beautiful here. He is treating me well. I just wanted to call and let you and everyone know I am doing great and made it safely. I wanted to speak to dad. Do you think you can go get him?" I asked.

"Yes. Hold on for a few minutes," she said. I heard some shuffling and noises before the phone went silent. I knew she had left the room. A moment later, I heard shuffling and noises again as the phone was being picked up.

"Patience . . ." Kyle's voice came on at the end. He sounded weary. When I didn't answer him, he spoke again, "Please talk to me. I need to hear your voice."

Titus's body went rigid as he listened. "Alpha, how are you doing?"

"Please don't say that. Call me Kyle. You used to call me that," he pleaded. His voice was broken.

"I prefer alpha instead," I replied calmly.

"It's Kyle, please. I miss you, Patience." Titus released a growl, and I moved to touch his chest where I began moving my hand up and down his body. Part of it to calm him down but I can't deny that I don't enjoy touching his hard chest.

"You have to stop, Alpha. This has to end. You have my sister. However, It's actually a good thing you picked up. Now that you have my sister, and I have my chosen, I think it is best if you and I should make a clean break. We can start out fresh," I began and Kyle interrupted.

"No. Don't do what I think you are doing," he retorted immediately. "I won't let you do it."

"I, Patience Valek, accept your rejection, Alpha Kyle from Greenwood Pack."

And it was like a string that snapped between us. I felt a pinch of pain in my chest from the break of the bond. It was the last of our bond completely letting go and I heard Kyle roaring on the other side of the phone. He was an idiot and to be quite honest, my sister deserved better than him.

"Patience, I am not letting you go. I am coming for you. I don't care about your sister or her feelings anymore," he said angrily. "You're mine! It was stupid of me to let you go. You are coming back home with me when I get there. I'll rip that ass—"

Titus stole the phone from me and placed it by his ear as he spoke threateningly. "Come for her and I'll kill you before you can cross my territory."

"She's mine!" Kyle roared on the other end.

"Not anymore. She isn't," Titus replied. "Now she is mine."

Kyle roared on the other end again, and I heard Kailyn shouting at him to stop. I heard noises and my father's voice trying to calm Kyle down. I no longer felt anything for him. The bond I had with him no longer existed, and the only bond visible enough for me was Titus. I felt relief for the first time in a long time. There was always this heavy weight on my shoulders and my heart was always in constant pain. I held onto Kyle and the bond because I had hope. Now, I realized it was useless to hold onto something that will never work. Kyle had made his decision. He can regret it all he wanted, and I knew for a fact I was doing the right thing for me.

The phone got picked back up and my father came on the other end.

71

"Patience, we have to let you go. I wish I can talk to you further but it looks like we have our hands full right now," he said quickly.

"What is going on?" I asked when I heard furniture crashing and things breaking.

My father raised his voice, "Alpha Kyle isn't handling the break of the bond really well. We need to control him. I can't talk right now but take care of yourself, child. I hope to see you soon."

"It's okay dad. I'll talk to you another day. I am sorry to have caused you any kind of trouble."

"Don't be sorry, Patience. This is not your fault. You have to remember that this is not your fault. Alpha Kyle did this to himself. He will just have to live with his decision. I stand by what you have decided. You are my daughter and I am on your side," he replied. "I have to go. I will talk to you soon."

After that, we hung up quickly. Titus wrapped his arms around me as he sniffed me to help calm him down. He was feeling on edge too probably due to the threat that was issued by another Alpha. It was a challenge and his wolf must be feeling on edge. I wrapped my arms around him.

I wondered what was happening back at home. Kailyn would know for sure this time if Kyle was creating this kind of ruckus. He needed to control his temper but then again, this does not involve me. It wasn't my job to care about what happens to Kyle or Kailyn. She was my sister and if anything, I do hope she would find out. I might have been a coward to not have told her but I really did want to protect her from any kind of pain.

Titus's rigid body was pressed against me. I sighed and pulled him closer, hoping to soothe away any kind of emotion he was feeling. This was tough on all of us. Finding a chosen like this was almost always a complicated matter. However, holding Titus in my arms was giving me strength to look forward to the future. I could see myself with him. He was a possessive and dominating alpha but he was also caring.

"I am happy that I met you, Titus," I whispered.

His body relaxed a little and his arms tightened around me. His nose and lips brushing up against my sensitive skin on my neck. It felt right in his arms.

"And I am happy that you chose me, Patience. If he comes for you, I will fight for you." His breath brushed against my skin, making me shudder. This tall domineering man was mine, and he was going to fight for me. I had someone to stand in front of me— a wall that would protect me. I felt safe.

CHAPTER 17

KAILYN

I heard commotion coming from the other room. It sounded like someone was getting hurt. Picking up my speed, I ran towards the noise. When I opened the door, I saw my dad and the beta nailing down my mate who seemed to look like a crazy male. He was growling like crazy and shouting that she was his. Deep inside of me, something tugged and I knew something was wrong—something I never bothered to look at or see. It was as if someone put a blind over my eyes.

Kyle looked furious and crazed. He had never shown me this side of him. With me, he had always been the calm and composed male that I knew he was. He never picked a fight with me. He gave me everything I wanted but that didn't stop the seed of suspicion.

"Kailyn, get out of here," my dad ordered when he saw me at the door entrance.

"But—" I started, wanting to help them. I was Kyle's chosen mate after all. I should be able to calm him down.

"Get out!" my dad commanded again in a firmer voice. It held no room for arguments. Even with my father commanding me, I hesitated. I glanced back at Kyle one last time as I didn't want to leave him. He needed me and I couldn't abandon him.

Kyle whipped around to look at me. His eyes were blazing with anger and fury I had never seen before. It was directed at me, "I don't love you. I thought I did. I love your sister. She's mine! She's my true mate and I lost her!"

The air in my lungs left me completely. I couldn't breathe. An immense amount of pain twisted in my chest. I felt my world spinning around me. Memories flickered through my mind—all those years of seeing Patience in pain, crying, and looking heartbroken. I never thought it was Kyle. Among all the males in the pack, it was him. I shook my head and Kyle looked at me, fuming.

"Yes, it's true. She's mine. I thought I loved you. I made a mistake. I need her. She's my rightful luna that the moon goddess gave me. I thought the bond with you would grow, but it didn't. I only grew to love your sister more and more." Each word was like a knife to my heart. Tears streamed down my face; I felt betrayal. I felt guilty for taking my sister's mate. It was beyond my imagination. I couldn't believe that without thinking, I had hurt the people I loved, and I didn't even know about it.

Why didn't Patience tell me?

Why didn't my parents tell me?

I felt stupid. I felt hurt and betrayed. How could they do this to me? I decided to live a life that wasn't mine but then the truth was I couldn't blame them completely, could I? It was my fault that I chose a chosen instead of waiting for my true mate.

The betrayal from my family was painful, but my stupidity also made me hate myself. I should've seen what was in front of my eyes. My dad looked at me from the ground as he pinned down Kyle. The concerned eyes of a father were looking back at me, but it only made me feel worse.

"Don't," he said quietly. "We did it because she wanted you to be happy. You were already with Kyle then. She didn't want to hurt you."

Clenching my first together to control my own emotions, I turned back to Kyle and truly looked at him. He spent his nights saying he loved me but it was all a lie—he didn't love me. I was a replacement for Patience. When we were making love, he never uttered a single word or any phrase of love.

Pain.

A sob left my lips and I quickly covered it with my fist. I didn't recognize the male in front of me. My whole life was a lie.

"You never loved me, did you?" I asked him. His eyes were still black but his shoulders drooped with guilt. His face told me everything I needed to know. If he did love me, he would have stopped me a long time ago.

"I did love you, but I can't fight what the moon goddess gave me. For years, I fought it thinking I was doing the right thing but for those years I have grown to love her more and more. I am sorry, Kailyn. I never meant to hurt you." His eyes started turning back to its normal color. His anger was slowly dissipating.

"But you did," I said weakly.

He pushed himself up onto his knees but my father and the Beta still had him firmly pinned. His arms were held in a tight grip to keep him down.

"Understand that I couldn't fight it. I was too weak."

"Did I ever mean anything to you? W-What we had was just an act? Did you even care about me?" It didn't matter now, but I needed to know if anything we had in the past meant anything. I didn't understand what he was going through because I never found my mate. Staring at him, I knew I loved him. The feelings and affection I carried right now were real. The pain felt like my heart had been broken into a million pieces.

"It was never an act u-until I found out that Patience was mine." He looked guilty. His eyes were desperate. "I loved you. I know for a fact that I did."

"You loved me but why didn't you give me up when you found Patience? Why did you lie? Why did you mark me when you knew that my sister was yours?" My pain was quickly laced with fury.

He looked down in shame. "I didn't want to abandon you."

"You took pity on me because I couldn't find my mate?" The shock and pain came roaring back. I took a step back. This was too much.

"Kailyn, please, listen to me." He pushed against my father and beta to stand up. "I'm sorry for what I did. I never meant to hurt you. You have to believe me. I did love you. I just know that I can't resist the bond any longer. Patience was meant to be mine."

Tears streamed down my face and the sudden surge of anger tore through me again. I glared at him with hatred. How could he sleep with me and speak of words of love to me all this time when it was all a lie? He stopped loving me the minute he knew Patience was his. He just never knew it but I know that he did. I had known Kyle for so long that I knew how his mind thinks before he does. It just amazed me that I didn't realize it until now. I guess I thought I did know how his mind worked. I gripped my hands tightly into fist. My fingernails dug into my palms but the pain was incomparable to what I felt in my chest.

"Sorry doesn't cut it, Kyle. You stay away from me and you stay away from Patience. She's happy now. Don't you dare go near her. You don't deserve her and you don't deserve me. As for what you and I have, we are done," I spoke through my tears, surprisingly calm. I looked at my dad who looked sad as he looked at me. I couldn't look at him. No. It would only break my heart even more. I spun on my heels and ran out of the office with one intention in my mind. I needed to get to Patience. I needed to apologize for all the pain I have caused her.

CHAPTER 18

PATIENCE

After my phone call with my family, I felt something was wrong. My guts were churning and there was a strange tug in my heart. I worried for my dad and my sister. I worried that Kyle might've told my sister who I was to him.

It wasn't fair. He didn't have the right to do that. He rejected me and now that I was finally happy, he was going to say that he wants me? He was selfish, a coward, and disgusting but then again knowing Kyle, I knew he would do whatever he wants to get what he wanted.

I understood that in a way, the fact that I hid what Kyle was to me from my sister was wrong. A *family* should have no secrets but who was I to demand my mate from my sister when she was clearly in love with him? Who was I to place myself in between what had been growing between them for years? Moon goddess might've chosen me to be his mate, but was the mate bond strong enough to fight against a chosen love? All I knew at that time was she was in love with him and their bond was stronger than mine, and I didn't have the heart to hurt my sister and destroy her love for Kyle.

Imagine my surprise when Kyle told me on the day Titus came to get me that he had fallen in love with me over the years. The idea made me snort in hilarity. It showed how selfish he was.

He dragged me on his side for years and kept my sister in his arms every night. It was perfect for him and he made his choice.

I should've told my sister then but everything happened so quickly. If I did not leave, Titus would take his Kyle's head. My phone call to was intended to speak with my dad regarding the issue of Kyle, but dimwit decided to pick up the phone and talk to me.

After the phone call, Titus left to speak with Christian while I was left wondering down the halls until I found myself in the back of the house. I had no clue how I landed myself here but at least I made it to the lower level. I found a group of young teen females laughing and giggling at Noor while training the pack warriors on the field.

Noor was walking around shirtless with his hands behind his back. He was cute with his tan skin and black hair tied into a ponytail behind his back. It made him look rugged with his broad tattooed chest. He had the darkest protruding brown eyes I have ever seen but I think that was his best feature because it made him look all the more dangerous. No wonder the young teen females were sniffing around him.

"Noor," I shouted as I made toward him. He turned around and smiled when he saw me.

"Patience, what are you doing out here? Where is the alpha?" he asked, looking around.

"He left me to speak with Christian. Honestly, I don't know how I landed myself out here. I was looking for the breakfast room," I replied and he began laughing as he shook his head.

"We need to give you a proper tour," he said.

"That we do. At this rate, I would get lost in a supply closet," I muttered. He grinned at my comment. "So it seems you have attracted yourself to a group of young females."

He turned to the group of girls and then back at me. "They do it every day."

"Do you have a mate, Noor?" I asked.

"Not yet but I do hope to find her soon. It would be nice to finally be mated to someone you are destined to be with," he said truthfully and I nodded. "So how about you and I—"

I was about to ask to join in on the training when I felt a pair of eyes burning through my back. I already knew who it was even before turning around. Titus was making his way down the hill, his forest green Henley stretched tight against his upper chest and muscular arms with his hand shoved into his jean pockets.

"Well, there he is," Noor said. Titus walked up to us a scowl on his face. When he came to my side, he placed a hand on the back of my head and placed his forehead on mine.

"Why are you always wandering off?" he whispered.

"Do you want me to remain in our room until you come back?" I said. I knew it wasn't going to happen. He looked like he was actually considering it so I changed the topic.

"I was looking for the breakfast room."

"You are far from it, *ma cherie*," he said.

"I didn't know where I was going so I walked around and ended up here," I responded. He broke into a grin and I could see the laughter reflecting in his eyes.

He sighed. "It seems we are in need of a tour of the pack house. I would ask someone else to do it but I think it is best if *I do it*."

He wrapped an arm around my shoulders protectively and headed up the hill as he spoke again, "By the way, your sister is on her way here."

My feet planted straight onto the ground and he stopped to look at me. My sister was coming? There it was again—the gut feeling something was wrong.

"Why?" I asked.

"I am not sure but your father called to inform us she left."

"Alone?" I asked.

"It would seem so," Titus replied but I could see how this was also affecting him. He was also wondering what was going on at my old pack. "I sent Christian to wait for her at the airport. She should be here in half a day."

I sighed. Something just kept gnawing at me. It felt like one of those feelings you get when you feel that trouble was just right around the corner.

"I hope everything is okay . . . maybe I should call my dad?" I asked.

He looked \ at me and sighed. "He is busy, mate. When a pack loses their luna, it is a total frenzy. Trust me when I say, we should wait for your sister for answers."

*　　*　　*

KAILYN

The moment I got off the plane and went through the narrow passage, I had no clue how to get to Patience's new pack. All I thought about was running away. I didn't realize what I was doing until I got here. Nervousness settled in as I hope someone here spoke English. I walked around until a scent hit me. My heartbeat quickened and my hands grew clammy. I tightened my hand into a fist as I felt a pair of eyes looking at me.

No.

This is not happening.

I maneuvered away from the eyes burning through me and began running. *I won't look back.* This was a nightmare and I needed to get away fast. It was bad enough that my chosen mate was Kyle— Patience's mate. To find my mate here was a cruel twist in fate. I would not do it. I couldn't do it because I was ashamed. I mated with a chosen instead of waiting. He deserves someone better. I saw a huge crowd and I knew I could lose my mate in that crowd as well as mix my scent enough to confuse him. I quickly headed into it.

My body rubbed against everyone else's as they moved in the same direction. When I emerged my eyes darted around seeking an escape. When I saw a dark hallway, I ran as fast as I could down that hallway and continued to make random turns until I found myself a door that was unlocked. Immediately I moved to open it, quickly darting into the pitch black room. I leaned against the doorway and clutched at my chest that was now aching.

Why did fate have to be so cruel and complicated? I was so ashamed of myself. The mistakes I have made and the truth that was hidden was killing me, and now I met the one thing that I never thought I would see.

Distantly, I heard faint footsteps and my body stiffened; fully alert that someone was getting closer. I quickly darted around the pitch black room, seeking a place to hide but tripped over a box and went flying down onto the ground. I covered my mouth from screaming as I felt pain shoot through my ankle. Getting up on my hands, I pushed myself back until I hit the wall away from the door and curled up my feet close to me as I waited. My heart was beating so fast against my chest. I think even the other person could hear it, human or not.

The footsteps stopped in front of the door I entered. *Oh no. Go away.* I held my breath as I waited for the other person to leave. After a moment, the footsteps started retreating, and I exhaled with relief. Crawling on my hands and knees, I made it to the door where I opened it slightly to peek out. The scent that hit me told me it was my mate tracing me. I swallowed hard as it was the most alluring scent I had ever smelt before. The ache in my chest stirred again. I would never be able to experience this and it was my entire fault. I had no one else to blame but myself.

I crawled out of the room and then using my hands, pushed myself up to a standing position—well, half standing up. I was leaning against the wall as my ankle was throbbing. It would take at least a few hours for it to heal.

"Damn it," I muttered. Moving slowly, I made my way to the information desk and asked for a phone so I could call Patience to come and get me.

My mate's scent still lingered in the air and I found comfort in it. My wolf was definitely happy. Her ears are perked and alert. She wanted to see him but she knew we didn't deserve to.

I walked for a little bit before I frowned and looked around. I had absolutely no idea where I was. I sighed and fell down on my butt as I was too exhausted to even continue. I sat down and looked down at my hands, contented in just sitting here and drowning in my misery with my mate's scent wrapping around me as I can smell he was just here.

A pair of white shoes appeared in front of me. I blinked a few times as I stared at it before my eyes traveled up from the shoes to meet the owner. What I saw took my breath away. The beautiful male standing in front of me was staring at me with an intense russet color eyes. The connection was instant and the pull was strong. I felt my soul literally being yanked closer to his. Subconsciously, I shook my head. *No.*

I began crawling away from him, but his hand came out to grab my shoulder, pulling me back against the wall again. I closed my eyes tightly, refusing to look at him. I could feel his breath on my cheek as his nose touched my face.

"You smell like another male but the bond I have with you tells me *you are mine,*" he said huskily His voice was controlled and steady which scared me. There was a hint of a threat behind it. I swallowed hard again.

"P-please, let me go," I whispered.

He chuckled wickedly, "Why would I do that, *mate?*"

"Because I am not y-yours," I said quietly even the words were hard to force from my lips.

I felt his hand on my cheek and then down to my neck. The instant cold and pleasurable tingles that spread from that touch had my body melting. It was nothing I have ever felt before. Even with Kyle, it wasn't like this.

"This tells me otherwise," he replied softly. Dear goddess, his voice was so deep and masculine it sent shivers through my body and goose bumps spreading all over my body. The way he had that French accent has me weak at the knees. "Open your eyes."

My shook my head and closed them tightly.

"Open your eyes, or I will kiss those luscious plump lips of yours right now," He demanded. His voice was hard with little patience and my eyes fluttered open immediately to look back into his eyes.

"You can't force me to do anything. I will have my sister's pack hurt you. They will find me. They live here," I threatened. He arched an eyebrow at me and it was the most sexiest thing I have ever seen. Damn him! Damn mate bond! Resist, Kailyn.

"Interesting," he murmured.

"Yes, her mate is the alpha! He will rip your head off if you force me to do anything I don't want to," I threatened angrily. "It's best if you let me go."

"Oh, what would be the fun in that? I think I quite enjoy the idea of taking you away," he said nonchalantly.

"Please just let me go," I tried again. "You don't want me."

His eyes darkened immediately to pitch black. "Don't speak for me. You don't know what I want."

I tore my gaze away from him with tears streaming down my face now. He moved to cup my cheeks so that I would look at him and his eyes were back to its normal color. His gaze softened as he saw tears running down my cheeks.

"I have been waiting for you for years. I am not going to let you go that easily, Kailyn," he gently spoke and my heart again came to a stop. How the hell did he know my name?

"H-how—" I began, but he interrupted me with a devilish grin.

"You look a lot like your sister. She hasn't met me but I have heard a lot about you two. Imagine my surprise when my mate comes stumbling to me," he said. I looked at him with my eyebrows furrowed, clearly confused.

"My name is Micah Beaumont, Alpha of Red Thorn."

CHAPTER 19

KAILYN

"I can't," I said quietly. "Please, just let me go."

Micah did not look happy. In fact, he looked furious. He moved to scoop me up into his arms. My arms quickly shot around his neck to hold on in case I fell.

"You aren't going anywhere," he replied. "I'm taking you back and if you think about leaving me, I won't hesitate to tie you to my bed."

I gulped and looked around for some kind of help. As if Moon Goddess above heard my prayers, a tall dark skin man appeared around the corner. His eyes immediately landed on us and a firm set line was placed on his face as he walked towards us with purpose. Micah noticed that I was quiet and turned to look.

"Well, Beta Christian, isn't it nice to see you here as well," Micah said nonchalantly.

"Very funny, Alpha Micah. Let Kailyn go," he ordered.

Micah arched an eyebrow before laughing. His chest rumbling against me. "You have no power to order me, Beta. Know your place. She's mine. I'm taking her back to *my pack*."

The tall dark man looked from Alpha Micah to me, and I could see the surprise in his eyes before he quickly masked it and turned back to Micah. His face was void of emotion. He looked very dangerous. In fact, both males in front of me were oozing with testosterone and male dominance.

"Who are you?" I asked. Micah growled lowly.

Beta Christian turned towards me, "I'm Alpha Titus's Beta. I was sent to retrieve you at the airport. Is it true that Alpha Micah is your destined mate?"

"No."

"Yes."

Micah and I both said at once. I turned towards him and he glowered at me. "Put me down."

Micah grinned at me. "I like it when you are feisty."

Oh dear goddess above, this male was really going to drive me crazy with those smiles. My mind fluttered back to Kyle and guilt set in. I couldn't do this to him, could I? Even with the things he had done, I couldn't fully blame him. We were both in love and he gave up Patience for me, but then again, he told me he wasn't mine. I gnawed at my bottom lip crazily, and I started to squirm in Micah's embrace as all this thinking was driving me a little mad.

"Stop moving," he barked. His eyes were still on Beta Christian.

"Alpha Micah, I will not leave him without her. My alpha will have my head," Beta Christian said as he moved closer to us.

"And I will not leave here without her and if that means ripping your head off, then so be it." He growled angrily back. I began rubbing his back in a consolation manner. I didn't realize what I was doing until Micah turned towards me. I stopped immediately and turned to Beta Christian.

"My sister is aware I am in Paris?" I asked.

He nodded. "I came to bring you to our pack but it seems we are in a predicament."

I turned back to Micah, "I will go with you but you have to do something for me first."

He eyed me suspiciously. I could see it in russet colored eyes. He was debating if he should take the bait and agree or if he should just rip off Christian's head off. I am pretty sure a big fight would break out as Christian did not look like an easy Beta to take down.

"What are you hiding in that pretty little head of yours?" he finally asked.

I sighed, "Nothing! I just want to go see my sister. I really do need to talk to her. We have so many things we have to clear up. You caught me in a bad time."

He looked at me warily before turning to Christian. "Very well. We will go to your pack. Inform your alpha of my arrival, and I will be bringing a few warriors with me as I am on your territory.

"You can come later but for now I will take Kailyn with me," Christian said. Micah snarled his response.

"No. She's mine and she is coming with me. You have my word, Beta. I will bring her to your pack."

*   *   *

PATIENCE

I stood in our bedroom, pacing as I waited for news of when my sister would get here. TItus sat on the bed watching me walk back and forth. After a while, he sighed and stood up as he walked to my side and wrapped his arms around me.

"Don't think too much. Christian will bring her back. I trust him," Titus said gently.

"I know. I am just worried about what happened at home. Can you call him again?" I asked turning to find comfort in his big arms.

He chuckled. "He will call when he has retrieved your sister."

"But that was like hours ago!" I said angrily.

He was about to answer me when the phone rang. We both turned towards it as it was on the bed. He let me go to grab it as he picked it up and listened to what they had to say he turned away from me as he spoke in french again.

Damn French language!I moved closer to see if I could hear more of what was going on but Titus had already hung up and turned towards me. His face remained passive, but his shoulders were tense. I could sense he did not feel easy about what he was going to tell me.

"What is it?" I asked. "Is it about my sister?"

"Christian went to the airport to go pick up your sister but it seems your sister had run into her destined mate there, and now Christian is coming back empty handed. Your sister and her mate will be arriving after Christian," Titus said.

"What? She found her destined mate? What about Kyle?" I asked. Titus turned sour at the mention of Kyle's name.

"Those answers I can't answer for you, *ma cherie*. You will have to wait until your sister arrives. It is her decision to choose her destined or chosen." He moved to pull me back into his arms as if the distance was unbearable. He sat on the bed and pulled me to sit on his lap.

"If she goes back to Kyle, then her destined will be mateless. If she goes with her destined, then Kyle will also be mateless," I said and frowned. Titus began sniffing my neck. His nose was trailing my skin like a feather, brushing gently.

"She is in the same predicament as you. If she chose her destined, will you go back to Kyle?" he asked and I could see how rigid his stance was as he waited for my answer.

Would I go back to Kyle? I didn't see that happening. My time with Titus had somehow strengthened my bond with him. Also, after the Moon Goddess visited me in my dreams, how could I turn my back on what she had given me? Although, I haven't figured everything out completely, I had a feeling that what she had given me had to do with Titus. His touch stirred a burning desire inside of me that not even Kyle's can compare.

With Titus, there was this tug the minute I saw him. The way my wolf instantly reacted around him told me, she also viewed him as her mate. Her allegiance with Titus shocked me the most. Everything with Titus was so much stronger at so many levels compared to Kyle.

"No," I whispered. I felt Titus relaxed a little before he kissed my neck and trailed up to my jaw line.

"Good. Because I would have to kill that mutt," he muttered and I couldn't help but smile. He was really a possessive and protective mate.

I moved to straddle him. It was the first time I initiated this kind of intimacy, but I really wanted to see his face. The way his icy blue eyes looked at me brought a shiver down my spine. His eyes were so intense and raw. I moved to cup his cheek. He didn't move a muscle the whole time. He sat frozen to his spot watching and calculating my move. I leaned down and began trailing kisses on his left jaw line up to his cheek and then chastely kissed his lips.

When I pulled back, I smiled with satisfaction but he growled and his hand came to the back of my head as he brought my lips back down to crush his lips against mine. Oh dear, that was a completely different kiss from what I gave him. His tongue darted out to lick the seams of my lips asking for entrance and my lips opened willingly. A throaty groan left his lips as his tongue slipped in immediately to claim and taste every crook in my mouth.

At first, I was unsure of what to do but soon, my tongue was playing with his fighting for dominance. He was relentless and demanded me to submit. When I didn't, he pulled my lower lip into his and gently nipped it. A small moan escaped my lips and a satisfied rumble came from Titus's chest. I melted in his arms.

He flipped us over like nothing as he maneuvered me under him—one hand in my hair and the other on my waist as he placed himself between my legs. His lips left mine and trailed down to my pulse where I felt him inhale sharply.

"Your scent drives me crazy," he whispered huskily. "It is something I never smelt before. It is so pure and sweet. It is taking all of my strength not to mark you yet."

"Why don't you do it?" I asked.

He licked my pulse and then I felt his canine graze my skin before he spoke again, "Because I want you willing. I want you to be all mine. I don't want you to doubt your feelings for me. When I mark you, you are mine forever. Your soul will be mine as mine is yours."

I knew what he said made sense. He wanted me to be sure that I didn't want Kyle because marking binds souls together for life regardless if the wolf is marked more than once. It binds their souls. The other side might lessen but the connection will always be there.

My hands were running through his hair. He was driving me crazy with his body heat and the bond between us was silently vibrating with our closeness. My eyes fluttered close when he licked a spot behind my ear.

A soft knock on the door pulled both of us out of what we were doing. My eyes opened, and I looked up at Titus whose eyes were black with desire and need. My body was responding automatically, and I wanted nothing more than to pull him back into my arms and start where we left off, but the knock again brought me back out of what I was thinking.

"Yes?" Titus barked impatiently. He moved down to kiss me one last time on the lips before pulling up quickly and began walking to the door. I didn't realize I was breathing heavily, and my heart was beating so fast until he was gone. I placed a hand over my heart as I turned to look at him as he opened the door.

"They will be here in less than a minute," Christian's voice came on the other end. I quickly sat up and scooted off the bed. I pushed Titus aside and opened the door wide enough to see Christian looking down at me.

"Is she okay?" I asked.

91

"She is fine," he replied with a grin. "Although, I think this is about to get very interesting."

"I have to go see her." I saw from the corner of my eyes that Titus tried reaching for me, but I quickly evaded his grasp and ran down the stairs without a glance back. I heard him shout my name but I didn't stop. I had waited long enough to hear from Kailyn.

When I arrived outside, a black jeep pulled into the driveway. The driver side opened and out came a tall lanky male while the passenger side door opened and a female who radiated with power also stepped out. She was beautiful as she wore a black tank top that revealed her toned and slim body. She lifted up her sunglasses up on top of her blonde hair as she stuffed her hands in her pocket. A sly, devilish smile crawled on her face as she saw me.

The back door opened and out came a tall handsome black hair man before he turned back in and pulled out my sister.

Christian and Titus were behind me now, and I was about to run to my sister when I heard a male growl behind me.

"Mine."

CHAPTER 20

PATIENCE

"Mine."

My head whipped towards the voice as shock settled in. Christian's eyes were black as he looked at the blonde woman who just stepped out of the vehicle. Christian's body moved with ease but with determination as he made his way over to the blonde woman, who was smirking as she watched Christian walk over to her side.

His hand moved to the back of her head and he placed his forehead on hers as he whispered again, "Mine."

"Yours," she whispered back. Gone was the smirk and in its place was a dazed look as she looked at Christian.

"Hold on." The male who was still holding to a struggling Kailyn frowned as he looked at what just happened. "No, not my beta."

Christian released a growl and his eyes darted to the male, observing if he was challenging him for his mate.

"She's my beta. If I lose her, I would have to find a replacement."

"You make it seem like it is the hardest thing ever," Titus's voice was a lot closer now to me. I felt his heat radiating through my back.

The male turned towards Titus as he grounded out. "Of course, it is hard to find a replacement. The one you chose for you is the best. I did the same."

"She's mine!" Christian roared.

"Let me go!" Kailyn's hand came up to grab at his hand that was wrapped around her wrist as she tried to pry his fingers away.

My attention diverted. I moved to my sister but Titus's hand came out to place on my shoulder, pulling me flush against his chest as he wrapped an arm around my front to keep me from moving further. I turned to him.

"He has my sister."

"He is Alpha Micah, your sister's mate. He will not harm her," Titus said, and I turned back to Kailyn who was looking at me pleadingly. This was a mess.

"Alpha Micah, if you would so kindly release my sister, I can assure you she will not run," I tried to reason with him. He narrowed his eyes on me to see if he could get some kind of read out of me. When he saw I was being honest, he nodded and released my sister, who came flying to my side.

"He's crazy!" Kailyn snapped angrily as she wrapped her hand around her wrist to ease the pain of his grip.

"Just don't run, mate," he chided as he walked over to us with the tall lanky man standing next to him. He turned to Titus. "Is there anywhere where we can talk?"

Titus nodded before he left he glanced down at me briefly before squeezing my body with his arm and then releasing me. After they left, Christian and his mate walked up to us. He was grinning.

"Patience, this is Beta Emily," he introduced me and I gave her a smile.

She looked at me curiously before smiling and moving in to hug me. I did not expect that. She looked bubbly and carefree, the total opposite of Christian. I wonder how he would handle his

94

mate. I was almost confident that he would have his hands full with her.

"It is so nice to meet you. Everyone around here has heard about your arrival. Alpha Titus is pretty famous with the females around here, being mateless and all. No females have ever gotten his attention until you," she said. "I can see why he picked you. You are absolutely stunning just like your sister."

I laughed softly, "Thank you."

After some talk, Christian and Emily left to spend time together. Kailyn turned towards me and hugged me tightly. After our hug, I pulled her back and led her back upstairs to my room. I didn't know where else to take her. If I even tried, I think she and I would end up in a supply closet.

"What happened?" I asked.

"I know about it, Patience. I know Kyle was your mate." I felt like my world came crashing down as I pulled her into my arms again.

"I am so sorry, Kailyn. I wanted to tell you so bad. You and I never keep secrets but you have to understand why I did it. You love him, Kailyn. I love you enough to want you happy," I said as a tear slipped from my cheek.

"I can see why you did it but why would you think I would want this? You are my sister! How do you think it made me feel to find out that I took my own sister's destined mate?" Kailyn reasoned as she pulled back and smoothed my hair behind my ear. "It destroyed me to realize that Kyle was yours. All those years, you were hurting. I didn't even stop to think that maybe he was yours. I am so stupid."

I shook my head, "Don't, Kailyn. We all had a choice and we all made it. Moon Goddess is either having a fun time playing with our destined mates or she had made a mistake because you have always loved Kyle. You should've been his destined mate, not me. Yes, I felt pain but Kailyn, I am okay now. Don't feel guilty. You have the right to choose."

She shook her head and tears began streaming down her face. "I can't. I feel torn. My heart feels like it is being ripped apart."

"You love Kyle still," I said quietly as I watched her pained face.

"I love him but I am feeling things with Micah that I have never felt with Kyle. It is like a spell that I can't resist. My soul is calling out to him," she admitted as she wiped her rosy cheeks from the tears that wouldn't stop spilling.

I didn't know how she felt. She and I might be in a puddle of mess but I never loved Kyle. I moved to grab her hands in mine.

"Listen, Kailyn. What do you think is the right thing to do?" I asked.

She sniffled and looked at me, her eyes brimming with tears. "I don't know."

"Get rid of all the guilt you have. Listen to your heart. What do you want? Do you want Kyle or do you want Micah?" I asked.

"Kyle doesn't want me, Patience.," she said quietly. Her voice sounded broken. "The reason why I left was because he told me he doesn't love me anymore. He has fallen in love with you. Even if I wanted him, he is no longer mine or the Kyle that I knew."

This was giving me migraine. I felt the vein on my temple pulsing, and I rubbed my temple to get rid of it. Kyle was being indecisive. One minute he would say he didn't love me, he loved my sister and the next, he told my sister he was in love with me.

"Then what are you going to do?" I asked. She looked at me again as fresh tears brimmed her eyes.

"I can't go with Micah. You need to hide me. You need to find a way for me to run away. I am not a good mate, Patience. I didn't wait for him. I picked a chosen who was my sister's destined mate—" she began but I interrupted her.

"You need to stop carrying around this guilt. This right here is not your fault. Our choices brought us here. If anything we are all at fault in some shape or form because of our choices," I said.

"I know that but I can't stop feeling this way. He is beautiful, Patience. I have never seen anyone as perfect as him but he and I are completely different.

I got marked by Kyle, Patience. I didn't even wait. I didn't even wait to think that maybe my destiny will show up any moment in my life. I gave up on my destined mate and went with my heart," she said dejectedly.

"Honestly, Kailyn, people make mistakes all the time. Nobody is perfect. I am not. Kyle isn't. We all made mistakes. You just need to forgive yourself and decide what it is that you want." I continued but I knew the reason why she was hesitant. Her human part was still in love with Kyle but her wolf yearns for her mate.

She stood up and began pacing. "It's not that easy. I am so torn inside. When I see Micah, all I want to do is jump his bones but when I think about that, I think about Kyle."

"Does Kyle want you?" I asked.

"No," she replied.

"Does he love you?" I continued.

"No," she replied after a moment. "But a part of me still loves him."

"Of course, you still do. He was someone important in your life. He played a part of your life for many years, Kailyn. If you didn't feel anything at all, I would say you have no compassion. He was your chosen. You have every right to feel this way but if Kyle doesn't want you, why go back to someone you said that told you he doesn't love you?" I reasoned.

"I don't know! I just need time. I need space. I need to get away." She whipped towards me. Her eyes were slightly wild as she spoke, "Please, give me a few moments alone to just think."

I sighed and nodded. Her face relaxed slightly. "C-can you take me away from him? I can still feel him close by and it drives me mad."

"Okay." I took her hand and led her down to the back door into the open clearing. Noor glanced up and saw us while he was still training. His eyes narrowed on Kailyn surprisingly. I waved at him before dragging my sister away from his view and down another hill and into the woods where we sat on a log.

We stared ahead of us at the nature in front of us, content in just watching what was going on around us. After a moment, Kailyn spoke up.

"How did we get here?" she asked with melancholy clear in her voice. I knew what she meant. We were always so close. Never in our minds did we think we would be in this kind of situation, but yet here we were. Fate was kind of cruel . . . well . . . I shouldn't blame fate when it was our choices that got us here, but who was to say that fate didn't play any part in this? I was talking in circles.

"I don't know but you and I can figure it out together. I am sorry, Kailyn."

"I am sorry too, Patience," she whispered.

We went silent for a while again before she spoke up again, "Let's forget things."

She stood up and began stripping. A grin came on my face as I knew what she was doing. I began stripping off my shirt and pants. When I was down to my bra and panty like Kailyn, we both started running and giggling as we went deeper into the woods and shifted into our wolves. Together, we ran for a few miles and allowed our wolves to play back and forth as siblings.

It had been a long time since we have done this together and to have our wolves to get in touch again was thrilling. We were so consumed in playing with our wolves we didn't realize how late it was until we heard paws hitting the ground and branches snapping. I stopped mid-jump to look around. Kailyn noticed my distraction and stopped as well.

Two large wolves came into view: Titus and Micah (I assumed.) They looked at us furiously. Kailyn looked at me as I looked at her. A slow wolf grin showed on her face and she burst into a run away from me. I knew what she wanted to do—her mischievous wolf wanted to play further. I ran the other way, and I heard Titus's wolf chuckle in the back as he followed after me. He seemed to become thrilled with chasing us. Out of the corner of my eyes, I heard and saw Micah growl angrily and ran after Kailyn.

I ran for a few miles and was able to dodge Titus's attempt in nailing me down until it went deathly quiet. I slowed down my pace to see if I could hear him as my ears perked up. I walked a few more steps before I was pushed to the ground. A whine escaped my lips as Titus sat on top of me. I tried pushing him off but he seemed content in just sitting on top of me as he nipped at my ear.

Damn him. He caught me.

*　　*　　*

KAILYN

I burst into a run, not wanting to go back to the mess I am to face yet. I could hear Titus's wolf chuckle and Micah's warning growl for me to not run. It sent a shiver through my body, and it only stirred my excitement more.

When I was training in my pack, I was one of the fastest wolves out there. I was also good at tracking. I wanted to see how bad this alpha was and just how much he would go. I didn't know if this was a good thing because it could lead to something bad, but I always liked a good challenge.

I heard him quickly catching up. He was faster than I thought. His wolf was bigger than mine so I could see why it didn't take much for him to catch me.

When he did, he pounced on top of me, and a growl escaped his lips. I snapped my jaw at his neck to get him off me but he only pinned me down harder.

We rolled around in the dirt trying to fight for dominance as he wanted me to submit to him, but I refused to do so which led me to my wolf angrily snapping at his neck to get him to lay off from me. The minute my canines sunk into his skin, I knew what I did. Panic set in, and I released his neck as I scrambled up onto my paws and stared at him in horror. We have started the mating process.

He shifted in front of me and clutched at his bloody neck, completely naked. His russet colored eyes were staring at me in shock.

No. No!

I spun on my paws and ran away from him. I heard him call out my name but I couldn't face what I just did. I was reckless and a mess. I couldn't believe I allowed my wolf's animalistic nature to take temporary control over my body that I totally forgot where I was, who I was, and what was happening. I was having too much fun playing around.

I realized it was too late because I could feel our bond strengthening. It was like light that was glowing brighter and a rope that was growing in length. I felt like I was grasping for Kyle's bond as I saw it slowly disappearing. The light was dimming slowly.

What have I done?

CHAPTER 21

KYLE

When Beta Roy and Patience's father nailed me down, I saw Kailyn running away from me. Reality began to set back in. My wolf whimpered inside me as he felt the loss of his destined mate and his chosen. My head was pounding and my veins were pulsing with adrenaline. My body slumped to the ground, and I felt Roy's hand relaxed on my back as well as Harold's.

"Are you okay now?" Roy asked. I grunted my response as I was far from okay. I was in constant pain. My heart felt like it was being ripped in two. My soul was torn. It was like walking through hot charcoal bare feet.

They pushed off me and stood close by watching my next move. I moved to kneel, my hands on the ground still and my head bowed.

Patience.

I made a bad decision and it cost me my destined mate. The only one I would have in my lifetime. I didn't know when I started loving her. I didn't even realize it until I lost her. Was it selfish of me to demand her to come back? I know it was. I was stupid for choosing her sister. I knew what I was doing right now was wrong. I knew what I was feeling right now was wrong.

The beast inside of me wanted to rip Titus's throat and mark Patience, but the human in me was reasoning for me to not do it. I failed her as a mate. She deserved to find someone who could love her, but even the thought of her with another had my skin prickling with hair as my wolf itched to come out.

I knew he didn't do it yet. The mating process hadn't started yet because I haven't felt anything, but I could feel my bond with her slowly disappearing. It was terrifying to me.

"Leave," I barked angrily. There was a brief hesitation. "I said fucking leave."

After a moment, their footsteps disappeared and the door closed behind me. I was completely left alone to wallow in my misery. I swallowed the large lump in my throat. My heart ached like a thousand knives were being plunged into it at once. Closing my eyes, I took a deep breath. I needed to clear my head. Heading over to my bookshelf, I took out a bottle of mind-numbing alcohol.

Taking off the cap I brought the copper glass bottle to my lips. The burning sensation was welcomed as it crawled down my throat. Plopping back down on my leather chair, I closed my eyes and allowed my mind to wander back to Patience.

She was always on my mind even when I told her I chose Kailyn.

She was always there.

I thought back to the day that I first found out she was mine. It was like a blindfold was lifted from my eyes when I saw her for the first time. She was the most beautiful creature and her sister's beauty dulled in comparison. Instantly, I was captivated. This might sound shallow but it was how I felt the minute I found out she was mine. At that moment, I knew I was in trouble.

I wanted her.

It led to me craving for her.

But . . .

I loved Kailyn. I loved her with all my heart. I loved her before and now. It was just a different kind of love. The door to my office cracked open, and I turned slightly to see it was Harold. He walked over and sat down in the chair across from my desk. His elbows propped on the arm rest and his hands folded in his lap as he looked at me.

"You are my alpha. I respect you. I have served your father and your father's father. I believe that your father has raised you to be a wonderful alpha, and I understand the decisions you have made. You have led our pack wonderfully and you are the mirror leadership of your father. This is what I think of you as my alpha.

As a father and you as my son in-law, I think of you as irrational, selfish, idiotic, and a cowardly male. You don't deserve my daughters. You don't deserve them. If you are going to choose one, stick with that decision. You don't get to jump from one to the other. They are sisters, for god's sake," he said calmly but as he neared the end, his voice rose to amazing heights and his body tensed with anger.

"I am sorry," I whispered.

"Is that all you have to say? You are sorry?" He growled out. "Well, sorry isn't good enough. I have stood on the side and watched you torture one of my daughters every single night and when she finally decided to move on, you turn your back on the other sister repeating the same action. Do you have no honor? Do you have no conscience?"

I knew he was angry and he had every right to be. Everything he said was right. I wasn't going to argue. I hurt them both with the decision I made. It was a wrong decision and decision cost me something important.

"You will not go near them," he threatened. "You are my alpha and I will respect you, but I am their father and I will do what I need to keep them safe."

"Harold, there is nothing I can say that will be enough to obtain your forgiveness. Hell, I don't think you should forgive me but you tell me what I did was wrong. I loved Kailyn. You saw how I loved her even before I found out Patience was my mate. I thought what I was doing was right. I didn't do it for selfish reasons. I did it because I thought that maybe, just maybe, I might have a choice in choosing who I wanted to spend my life with. Turns out, Moon Goddess is much stronger than I thought.

I get it, Harold. I should've waited. I should've not fallen in love, but can you really stop what the heart wants? I felt it in my heart. I felt my love for Kailyn. I can't even begin to understand how all this happened!" I thumped my chest hard as I shouted. The veins in my neck made an appearance as my emotions were on high. "I loved her!"

Harold sighed and leaned back down in his seat. He unraveled his hand and brought one hand up to his forehead as he rubbed his temple with his fingers. My grip on the bottle had tightened slightly, and I inhaled sharply before exhaling slowly.

"You made stupid decisions," he muttered.

"You don't have to be the one to tell me that. I know I am," I replied back wryly.

"What are you going to do now?" he asked as he glanced up at me.

"I don't know," I muttered as I lifted the bottle up to take a long swig.

"Kailyn left to go to Paris," he said and I choked on the alcohol and began sputtering.

When I finally got in control of my coughing, I turned to look at him. This old male did that on purpose. I could tell it by the smug expression on his face. I couldn't figure out if I wanted to punch him or strangle him.

"What the hell?" I gritted out.

"She said she wanted to see Patience."

"And you just let her go?" I asked as I began standing up. This was getting out of hand. I didn't expect for Kailyn to leave too. I stood up immediately as I had one thing on my mind and that was to go to Paris.

I heard Harold's voice behind me calling me to stop. My feet slowed down as I neared the narrow marbled stairway. I turned around to see Harold quickly catching up.

"You cannot leave," he said.

"Why the hell not?" I growled out.

"You are alpha! You have a pack to lead. They have already lost their luna and for their alpha to go running to Paris, how would that make things look? The council will have a fit about your position as alpha and your every action will be looked at. Think, Alpha Kyle," he said urgently.

My mind and heart were in chaos but my duty as an alpha requires me to stay. My wolf listened and agreed with Harold. I had no choice. I had to stay but as soon as things settled down here within the pack, I would be flying to Paris.

Growling angrily, I whipped around and headed down the stairs. Pulling my shirt over my head and throwing it on the ground, I broke into a run when I opened the front door and shifted mid-air. I needed to get rid of the tension and stress that was vibrating through my veins. I ran for hours and killed for my own pleasure.

It wasn't until I reached a clearing where the moon was shining down brightly that I stopped completely. My paws moved slowly through the tall grass as I looked around and sniffed the air. After a moment, I knew it was safe. My paws moved around the tall grass until I found a comfortable spot where I laid down on my belly and rested my head on my paws. I stared up at the moon as my eyes began to flutter close, taking my back to my comforting darkness.

CHAPTER 22

TITUS

"Titus, you can't sit on top of me like you did earlier!" Patience demanded as she finished putting on her clothes and slipped on her shoes. She turned to look at me with a frown on her face.

"What? I thought I saw something dangerous and so I did what any other male wolf will do. I protected what was mine," I reasoned as I slipped on a pair of shorts. I walked up to her and wrapped my arms around her. "Admit it though, you liked my wolf and I on top of you."

She blushed and tried to escape from my embrace. I looked down at her and saw a faint blush on her cheeks. She moved her dark brown hair behind her ear and bit her plump lips shyly. She was adorable and sexy. Ever since, I picked her as my chosen, I never felt anything like this before. I did a little research and found out that there was very little explanation on what was happening. Never in my years of being Alpha have I encountered this sensation I felt when I touched Patience or the bond that her and I had.

It has grown incredibly and my feelings were magnifying fast. It was so strong that when I look at Amelia I see and feel nothing. There was still that little dimmed bond I have with her but it was nothing compared to what I felt for this female in my arms. I moved one of my hands from her back to move her hair behind her ear. She glanced up at me curiously.

"You are beautiful," I whispered as my eyes again dropped her to lips that formed into a pout.

"You keep saying that," she replied and struggled to escape.

"It is because you are beautiful, mate. To me, you are the most beautiful female I have ever laid eyes on. Remember that," I retorted and the corner of her mouth lifted.

"You are beautiful too," she said and I frowned. I do not like being called beautiful. It is not manly. Men are not beautiful. Her lips lifted into a grin, and I moved to nip her lower lips.

"You are teasing me," I whispered against her lips before my tongue slipped out to lick her tasty sweet lips.

"Teasing? Never," she said a little breathless as her voice dropped completely into a low huskiness that turned me on. I tightened my arms around her.

"Careful, mate, you don't want to mess with an alpha. I might just eat you alive," I said as I moved to her ears and nipped at it hard. She yelped and struggled out of my embrace. My canine elongated, and I moved down to the crook of her neck. Her breath hitch and she froze.

"What are you doing?" she whispered.

"Teasing my mate," I responded nonchalantly.

"Patience!" Her sister's voice came from behind me. I sighed and dropped my forehead onto her shoulder.

Why does everybody always find the need to interrupt us?

"Kailyn, what's wrong?" Patience pulled back from my embrace to go over to her sister. Kailyn's face was pale as ever. I glanced behind her to see what caused her reaction. When I saw Micah following her with a fresh mark on his neck that looks too huge for a human bite but huge enough for a wolf bite, I turned back to Kailyn.

"I marked him."

107

"You what?" Patience exclaimed as she glanced behind and saw what I just saw.

I moved to rub my forehead. Micah walked up to my side and spoke. His face held a determination that I knew all too well. He and I might not be close but I knew his rule as alpha. He was an alpha of his word. He won't back down without a fight. In fact, he would l be a very strong ally. With him being my neighbor was a lot harder for rogues to slip through.

"You know our werewolves laws, Alpha Titus," Micah stated simply. He didn't look angry. In fact, he was a little smug as he looked at Kailyn who turned to glare up at Micah.

"Why should I go with you?" Kailyn asked. "I already have a mate."

"One whose bond can easily be ridden of," Micah growled possessively.

"Why are you being so difficult?" she asked with exasperation on her face as she turned to look at him. He growled and pulled her into his arms.

"Don't you think this is hard on me? My destined mate, the one who should've waited for *me,* was marked by another male? Don't you think I want to rip his throat out? Don't you think I want to drop you and leave you like nothing? I can still smell him on you. Do you know how hard this is for me too?" he growled angrily.

Kailyn's face fell and her tears began slipping quickly and fast. "I know. I am a horrible mate. This is why you should do exactly what you want to do. Leave me. I am not good for you."

Micah moved his hand behind her head and brought her forehead against his. "But I don't want to. I feel angry and I have every right to be but you are mine still. I won't leave you even if you told me to. I can have hundreds of females but I only get one of *you.*"

Kailyn sniffled and wiped away her tears. "Even when I am tainted goods?"

"Even then," he whispered back, and a slow smile slipped onto her face. "You're mine forever, Kailyn."

Kailyn's face softened and all worried slipped from her face. She wrapped her arms around him finally. Micah sighed and wrapped his arms tighter around her.

"I am sorry, Micah. I should've waited for you," she whispered with regret.

"I could understand why you did it," he replied. "Come on. Let's go back to the pack house."

Micah and Kailyn walked together back to the pack house. My attention flew back to my own mate who was standing in front of me staring at her sister. She was a tiny female. She only reached my chest and her tiny slender frame made her almost look fragile, but that was deceiving because her stance and muscle toned body told me she has worked hard at training.

Her body and the aura radiating out from her told me she was born to be a Luna. She turned around to look at me looking a little worried. I walked up to her and wrapped one arm around her shoulder as I led her back to the pack house. We had been outside in the woods far too long. I have avoided alpha duties to play with her and I assumed I was needed urgently back.

"What are you thinking?" I asked.

"It seems Kailyn has agreed to become Micah's mate," she said. "But what about Kyle?"

A possessive and protective emotion rose inside of me. I tightened my hold around her shoulders, pulling her closer.

"I don't know but it is what Micah had said. His mark on her will get rid of her chosen's mark. Her bond with her destined will be much stronger."

"I just hope . . . I just hope Kyle will be okay," she whispered.

An angry growl escaped my lips. I stopped my footsteps and turned us to face each other.

109

"You don't need to worry about another male, especially your destined. I am your mate now."

She removed my hands and took a step back. "Titus, he might've made bad decisions in the past but that does not make him a bad person. We all have made mistakes. I know Kyle as my alpha and he is a fair and good alpha."

I didn't like hearing that. In fact, I hate hearing everything about Kyle. I didn't know if it was the beast inside of me, but it made me more furious that she was defending him. I growled out angrily as my skin prickled with hair.

"He might be as you say he is but that doesn't mean I have to hear you talk about him," I reasoned and she huffed as she crossed her arms under her chest.

"Titus," she said my name softly and it was as if she placed me under her spell.

"What?" I muttered feeling my anger dissipating.

"I won't go back to him. I am yours," she reassured me gently, and I sighed and moved to wrap my arms around her, feeling her closeness was reassuring to my wolf and me. I didn't know what to do without her.

When we made it back to the clearing, Christian was waiting for me on the edge of the hill with Noor. Noor glanced down at Patience before looking back at me. When we arrived at their side, Noor spoke first.

"Well, we almost sent out a pack of warriors after you," Noor said, chuckling. Patience blushed slightly.

"I am sorry to have worried everyone. Kailyn and I just wanted to spend some alone time together," she spoke with guilt and Noor shook his head.

"Don't be sorry. We are glad you are okay," he said.

"Thank you," she replied and then glanced at Christian. "I am assuming you would be wanting a mating ceremony soon?"

Christian glanced down at her with his copper brown eyes, a slow grin made it onto his face as he remembered about his mate. "Yes. She will be staying. I spoke with her."

I nodded. "That's good. It is good to have two strong betas. Imagine the pups you will be having. They will be strong."

At the mention of pups, Christian's eyes glowed and his smile grew. "I can't wait, Alpha. The mating ceremony had to begin soon."

Patience softly laughed beside me and my gaze flickered to her. She was really beautiful when she smiled, and I loved that about her. She was completely different from Amelia. There was no way in hell I was going to lose her. I moved closer to her. Her presence always seemed to soothe me.

"Then a mating ceremony had to be planned," she answered with a smile.

CHAPTER 23

PATIENCE

A few days later, Kailyn and Micah had made up, and I was starting to see Kyle's mark on Kailyn's neck fading away. They were sitting in two white chairs whispering into each other's ears. A traditional mating ceremony doesn't start until the sun has fully set and the moon is high in the sky. It involved females wearing dark red gowns that touched the ground and males shirtless revealing their pack tattoos on their upper body-under the moon the tattoos shine back proudly at moon goddess.

When a pup shifts for the first time, their body will start to form a tattoo. By the time they are ready for training; their body will already take shape enough to reveal which pack they are from. When werewolves' switched packs due to moving to their mates' pack and perform the mating ceremony, their tattoo would shift that night to symbolize they are in their mate's pack.

"Are you ready, *ma cherie?*" Titus huskily whispered from behind me. His finger was trailing from my open back at the curve to my shoulder blade. Every touch it left a burning trail and it seemed to intensify more each time. A soft moan escaped my lips, and I felt his lips on my neck.

"Titus, behave," I whispered weakly. I could feel his grin. His hand slipped around from my shoulder blade to my shoulders and with a jerk, pulled me flush against his body.

"*Ma belle*, do you truly want me to behave?" He nipped at my neck. I tilted my head to the side to give him better access.

"If you don't behave, *mon loup* (My wolf), I will make it harder for you to chase me." I pulled away from him before turning to look at him, one hand still holding his by the finger tip. His eyes darkened with lust and determination. I batted my eyes in what I hope was flirtatious and licked my lips.

"If you are able to catch me, *mon loup*, I will let you kiss me." I continued feeling my heart pick up in speed at the mere anticipation of him catching me.

The corner of his lips lifted and his eyes twinkled with mischief. "That is a challenge, I will accept, *ma cherie*. You don't know what you got yourself into."

I was about to pull away but he yanked me back into his arms. His hand was sneaking around my waist as he leaned down and trailed hot kisses down my cheek to my neck.

"I love it when you speak French," he murmured, pressing his hardness against my belly. Heat pooled between my legs and I heard Titus's sharp intake of breath as he smelt my arousal. A rumble came from his chest. He pulled back immediately and began moving to the stage with urgency as he wanted to start the mating ceremony already.

"Good evening, everybody," he spoke with ease but his eyes trailed to me again, and I shifted under his gaze. It was hot and lustful. "Tonight, we celebrate the mating of Beta Christian and Beta Emily. It is a union that is welcomed and given by the Moon Goddess. For females who have their mates, get ready as you will be shifting in five minutes. You have two minutes to run as your mate will immediately shift at the two minute mark and runs after you."

Kailyn moved to stand next to me. Micah moved to stand with the rest of the other mated males who were looking at their mates with excitement and anticipation. Titus's gaze moved back to me. His eyes held a promise only he and I knew.

"He looks like he is going to eat you up," Kailyn murmured. I jabbed her on the side. Titus caught that little action and broke into a grin.

Confident, egoistical alphas!

"Hurry, let's go." I grabbed her hand and we moved to the line where all the females stood. I caught a glance of Amelia glaring at me from the sidelines. She was dressed in white as she did not have a mate.

I led the female packs as I stood a foot ahead of all of them. When the minutes began counting down, I risked another glance at Titus who was still staring at me. When he caught me looking, he winked.

Damn him.

He was distracting me. I needed to focus. I needed to make this extra hard on him. I slipped on a sly grin and turned back to him as an idea came to my mind. The minutes began counting down and when it reached its last fifteen seconds, I began lifting up my dress up to my thighs. The females caught onto what I was doing and they all gave a laugh as they began doing the same. The males were growling their displeasure and also eagerness to get to their mates.

When it reached one, we all burst into a run. I heard Kailyn giggling next to me. When we reached the edge of the woods, I lifted the dress completely off and shifted. My paws hit the uneven soft ground as I began the run. Some females followed alongside me as we moved deeper into the woods as others separated themselves.

When we heard the howls of our mates' excitement, we howled back our answers in return. Soon, I was left alone roaming the edge of the territory. When I saw a movement to my left, I didn't wait to see who or what I was. I burst into a run and flew past some logs. A familiar growl behind me told me it was Titus. He was quickly catching up. I needed to evade him. By my listening, I knew he was close. When I heard his paws dug into the ground I darted to my right. A wolf laugh escaped when I saw him slam into the ground face first.

I barked at him before running back in the opposite direction. I heard a river nearby and ran towards it. Hoping the air of the water would mask my scent. When I reached the river, it was unusually fast. I moved towards a fallen log that was hanging over the water as I began making my way to the middle of the fallen log. I stood on top of the log as I glanced down at the fast current. A snap in the log had my eyes darting back to the root of the log. When I saw that it was falling apart under my weight, I began making my way back. A yelp escaped my lips, and I fell headfirst into the fast current.

I tried paddling back to shore but the current was too fast. I shifted immediately after I realized that my wolf form would not keep me from drowning. With my arms, I began swimming towards shore but with the current pushing, it was a lot harder than I thought.

"Help!" I shouted, hoping that Titus was nearby. My arms were aching.

The burning in my muscles were killing me, and I could feel myself being pulled under more and more as I grew weaker and weaker.

"Patience!" Titus roared as I saw him running with a few pack warriors alongside the river a few yards behind me.

"Titus!" I shouted back, grateful that he was here. "I don't think I can hold on much longer."

"Hold on! I'm coming in!"

"What no! You are crazy! Stay out there! The current is too fast!" I managed to squeeze out with a mouthful of water. My arms cramped and I couldn't move anymore. My body gave up and I felt myself going under. I held onto whatever air I had left.

My eyes were beginning to hurt as my lungs squeezed me painfully for air. I opened my mouth on impulse as my body begged for air and my brain wasn't listening. I gulped down a bunch of water in response and my nose canal burned at the water that was inhaled.

I was going to die.

And Titus wouldn't get to even mark me.

This was my life.

Now that I was dying, I regret not telling him to just mark me.

I thanked the Moon Goddess for giving me a second chance and my parents for giving birth to me. I thanked for having a good sister, and I wanted to say that I lov—a strong pair of arms wrapped around my waist and pulled me against a hard chest. My head peeked up for air and I gasped desperately.

"Hold on," I heard Titus struggled to keep his weight and mine on top of water. If I struggled in his arms it would bring us both down. So I allowed him to take me where he wanted. I felt one of his arms leave my body and slowly we were brought back to shoreline. I fell onto the dirty ground, gasping and coughing. Titus immediately came to my side and hit my back with his palm.

"You are going to bruise my back," I muttered in between coughs.

"I need you to breathe," he said hoarsely. I turned slightly to look around and saw that his pack warriors have left. It was only him and me. I threw myself into his arms. He wrapped his arms around me, and I began crying like a little baby. The emotional turmoil that was ripping through me had me terrified and I needed contact. I gripped his body tightly in mine. He moved me so I was sitting in his lap as he rocked me back and forth.

When I was done crying, I pulled back and looked up at him. Fresh tears welled up as I saw the concern in his eyes.

"You are okay," he reassured me for the hundredth time.

"Where is everyone?" I asked.

"They all went back to finish the ceremony," he replied back calmly. His body heat was seeping into mine and I welcomed it with open arms.

116

"Should we go back?" I asked.

"If you don't want to yet, we don't have to." His thumb came out to wipe away a tear that had slipped out.

"I thought I was going to die," I whispered to him. His face was only inches away from mine. "I didn't think it would break on me."

"I know," he replied. I swallowed hard as I said the next thing that was on my mind. All I could think about was him and me and how I wouldn't finish what I wanted to do with him. Nothing was going to stop me now. This was going to happen now.

"I want you to mark me."

CHAPTER 24

PATIENCE

He didn't mark me. We ended up going back to the ceremony later. He was right not to though. If I really think about it, it was Christian and Emily's ceremony. This was about them. My mind was clouded with a near death experience that I didn't realize what I was asking of him. He wanted to wait till the time was right and he was completely right.

I had slipped back on my red dress and was walking back inside the home when I was yanked to a dark corner. My eyes adjusted to the dark and saw that it was Amelia. She was glaring up at me as she looked me up and down.

"Well, don't you look nice in red? I thought I told you he was my mate," she said maliciously. Her eyes narrowed into slits and her lips pulled back to bare her canine.

Well, this was certainly different from her sobbing.

"You like it? Red tends to make my skin glow and my eyes stand out," I replied back nonchalantly, completely ignoring her last statement.

A snarl left her lips and I arched an eyebrow.

"He's mine!" she growled out. Her hands curled into fist at her sides.

I heard faint voices coming inside the pack house. I moved a step away from her. "If that is all you are going to talk about, I suggest you stop wasting your breath. He is mine."

Her eyes flashed black and she let out an angry growl. "If you think that I would let this go easily you are mistaken. He is mine and I will have him back."

My back stiffened and my arms prickled with hair. The challenge was left hanging in the air and my wolf wanted blood. I rolled my shoulders to get rid of the tension and in a slow predatory stalk I walked over to her where I gripped her jaw with my hand. My face was mere inches from hers.

A slow sly smile slipped on my face. "Try it. I will enjoy killing you."

The grip I had on her tightened harshly as I was still raging inside. The balls she had to speak to me this way and to want to take back what she threw away. My wolf wanted to kill her but I didn't want to be irrational. Although I would enjoy killing her, I knew it would be a bad image for their future luna to kill Amelia—a pack member and their alpha's destined mate. It would make me look like the bad guy.

I pushed her away with a flick of my wrist and she went stumbling back, holding onto her cheeks as marks of my fingers still remained on there. I turned around and instead of heading up to the bedroom. I walked to the training room. I needed to get rid of the energy coursing through my body or I won't be able to control myself. I went into their closet and found some of their spare clothing that they leave in here and put them on.

Tying my hair into a ponytail, I went to the boxing bag and began punching it. I was not going to lie, I was imagining Amelia's face and it only made me punch harder. I was sweating and huffing by the time I slowed down. I placed my hand on my knees to control my breathing.

"What are you doing?" Titus's voice came from the entrance.

119

I glanced over at him. He had changed into his sleeping pants and was now shirtless. His tattoo spreading all over his chest like a dangerous male he stalked towards me. I pursed my lips and began punching the bag again. Seeing him so fucking hot was driving me insane and it made me think of Amelia.

"Are you going to answer me, Patience?" he asked impatiently. .

"No," I retorted.

He moved to hold the bag in front of him as I continued punching. His eyes roamed my sweaty body hungrily before coming back up to look at me.

"You're angry," he replied.

I punched harder this time just to send him back a few steps. He let out a grunt at the impact.

"Why?" he asked.

"It's nothing," I muttered and punched again.

"Then why are you punching a bag in the middle of the night?" He continued to prod. I stopped mid-punch to glare up at him.

"Can you just leave me alone? I want alone time," I said. He dropped his hand and the punching bag swayed back and forth as it lost what was holding it steady. I looked swayed for a moment before glancing at him. He moved closer to me this time. His fingers traced my jaw.

"Tell me."

"Stop it," I replied and tried to move around him but he wrapped his arms around my waist, pulling me flush against his naked chest. "I'm sweaty."

"I like it. Your scent is stronger. I can smell your adrenaline and how sweet you will taste. It's intoxicating," he murmured against my ear. My body shivered in under his teasing and I felt my anger slowly leaving my body. His touch was calming me down and placing a new heat in my body.

120

"Are you mad that I wouldn't mark you?" he asked. His hand was caressing my body, touching me in ways that had my blood on fire with a burning desire. The touch and grope me possessively. He made sure to cup my breasts firmly in his palms, claiming them without words.

"No," I whispered weakly. My will to maintain control was slowly slipping. I can never fight against the feel of his hands. They were heaven and the way he touched me made me feel like I am the only thing he will adore.

He moved to lightly suck on my neck. His tongue flickering back and forth on my sensitive skin. His breath spanned my skin and his arms tightened around me. I can feel the firm hard member of his pressing against my bottom. The sensation and core clenching desires was enough to have me roll my head back and knees weak. The ache between my legs was increasing. The thing he did to me was mind-boggling. I couldn't even comprehend how strong our bond was. It was kind of scary on how fast I felt for this male. In comparison to Kyle, Titus made me feel things I had never felt before. Now I barely feel anything for Kyle which was unnerving. I was falling fast.

Enough, Patience. You can play this teasing game too.

I turned around in his embrace and wrapped my arms around his neck, jumping I wrapped my legs around his waist. His hand came out to grab my bottom immediately to prevent me from falling. My lips came crashing down on his and I bit his lower lip before sucking on it apologetically. My tongue slipped out and delved into his mouth as I tasted him. There was this animalistic hunger that stirred up inside of me. My wolf was already on edge at the threat that was given from Amelia. The thought of losing Titus was enough to drive us to want to kill and now that he was here I *needed* him.

"I know you said you won't mark me but that doesn't mean you and I can't do other things," I whispered against his lips.

He hesitated and his body stiffened. I kissed him hard this time and rubbed my core against his hardness.

"Please," I pleaded softly. It was like The Great Wall of China was crumbling down to the ground. His body relaxed. He started moving. In moments, we were upstairs in our bedroom. He laid me down gently on the bed as he pulled back to look at me.

"Are you sure?"

"Yes," I replied instantly. His lips came back down on mine with determination.

His hands moved up from my stomach to cup my breast over the sports bra. I moaned and arched my back. His tongue was playing and teasing mine in a way that drove me a little mad. His hand moved up and slipped over the top of my bra to cup my breast in his hand and the contact was sheer pleasure. The heat and tingling sensation only deepened.

"Titus, please," I whispered against his lips. He growled lowly as his chest rumbled with need. His claws came out and he ripped my shorts in one swipe and my bra with the other. I was now completely naked underneath him. He took his time looking at me from top to bottom. His tongue darted out to lick his lips as he saw my glistening core. The action sent a jolting shock through me and I found myself needing some kind of relief from what was twisting inside of me.

His mouth came down on my lips as he kissed me hard. "God damn it. You're beautiful. Every single part of you is delicious and I can't wait to taste you."

I could only respond with a moan as his lips moved to my neck where he sucked on his earlier love bite. My hands went into his hair to tug on it. My claws were lightly scraping his scalp as I felt my wolf now on the surface. He groaned in response and nipped at my neck before moving down to the valley of my breast where he licked. I gasped at the new sensation. It was like he awakened my skin and it became alive as he touched it. His mouth moved to one of my breasts as he took in one of my nipples.

Oh dear goddess.

I mumbled a bunch of incoherent words and clung to his body like he was going to leave me any minute. The warmth of his mouth and his tongue playing with my breast had me writhing under him. He moved to the other where he paid the same amount of attention.

"Titus, goddess, Titus," I kept mumbling. I didn't realize where his hand was going until I felt his hand touching my most sensitive spot. I buckled immediately and arched my hip for more as a new sensation spread through my body.

His fingers slipped inside of me, and I couldn't find any words to describe what I was feeling and the moment it started moving, I was in a wild state. I brought his lips back up to mine as I kissed him hungrily—showing him just how much I need him, how much I crave for his touch. He growled out as he kissed me back just as much.

He moved to pull down his pants as he crawled back into bed and in between my legs. I knew what was going to happen next. I stared down at his hard arousal. It was thick and large. It was scary to look at it. I don't know if it will fit and nervousness sets in. His lips came down on mine as he kissed me this time gently.

"I will try to be gentle," he whispered.

I nodded and moments later, I felt him slowly entering me. The discomfort began spreading as he moved deeper. When he reached my hymen, he thrust hard. I cried out and scratched at his back. He moved to grab my hands and placed them on the sides of my head as he looked down at me. His eyebrows furrowed in concentration and his eyes filled with concerns. He was biting his lip to maintain control.

The ache was still there. I could still feel him inside of me. It was like a bad searing pain. A tear slipped out from my eyes. He moved to kiss it away and then pulled back.

"I am sorry," he whispered.

"I-it's ok," I said hesitantly. His hand moved down to where we were connected as he touched me again. The pain was quickly replaced with the pleasure I felt from earlier. I moaned and began grinding my hips. Surprisingly, I didn't feel the pain anymore. In its place was something else. A sound escaped as I tightened my legs around his waist.

He began moving, and I thanked him silently as it was just what I needed. His thrust was slow and gentle. His hand was still on my wrist besides my head. His eyes closed tightly. When what was building inside of me was reaching a point where I couldn't stand it any longer. I began wiggling underneath him.

"Titus," I whispered.

His eyes flew open and he gazed down with desire-filled black eyes. I pleaded with my eyes and he began moving faster. His thrust began to be more demanding. I tossed my head back and rolled my eyes back at the new sensation that hit me. I curled my hands into the sheets and my heels dug into his bum. He groaned and his thrust became more crazy and uneven. I was moaning like senselessly and my hands shot out of the bed to grip his hair in a desperate attempt to stay sane. I pulled him down for a harsh, deep kiss. He seemed to like that and his thrust spurred into a sexual frenzy. Whatever was tightening inside of me, broke.

Something snapped inside of me, and I let out a cry as his lips remained on me, eating up my cry of pleasure as if he only wanted him to hear them. No one else was to hear what was only for him. His thrust became harder and faster.

It hit so deep inside of me, I cried out for the second time as I felt myself release what was building inside of me again. He let out a growl and thrust many times as I felt him shoot his release deep inside of me. He continued his thrust until he was done. Sweat covered our body and the smell of our mating was thick in the air.

When he pulled back, his eyes were still glassy with desire and his eyes roamed my body hungrily again. He leaned down to kiss me one last time, greedily.

"Qu'est-ce que je ferais sans toi? Tu me rends fou (What would I do without you? You drive me crazy)," he whispered and kissed me one more time. "You are mine, Patience."

CHAPTER 25

KYLE

I was in the middle of training when I felt a sharp jab in my stomach that crawled all over my skin. It was like someone was skinning me alive. I dropped immediately to the ground. Everyone came running and my vision began blurring as the pain was unbearable. A cry left my lips.

Patience.

The only person that ran through my head. The only thing that stirred up an emotion so raw inside of me. I shook my head. This was not happening.

No.

My pack came running towards me. Beta Roy hooked my arms over his shoulder as he carried me inside to the bedroom. Tears streamed down my face. I cried for the loss of the bond. I cried for the loss of Patience. I cried for my sorry life. I cried because I felt as empty as ever even when I could still faintly feel her. It was the weakest bond ever.

Roy placed me on the bed. I rolled around in it for what seemed like forever until I fell asleep in exhaustion.

When I woke up, I was alone in my room. The pack house was dark. I stared blankly up at the ceiling, fighting back the tears that threatened to slip.

I was an alpha.

I do not cry.

I will not shed a tear.

Even then, I felt the hot tears sliding down the corner of my eyes. My life was crumbling before me. I stayed because of my duty as an alpha. I couldn't leave my pack stranded. They were my family but because of another decision, I lost the chance to possibly stop something that could be prevented. My heart was twisting with so much pain inside of me.

"Patience," I whispered her name and even then it hurt. "Goddess, why?"

Anger rose inside of me. I was angry with what has happened in my life. I was angry at the fact that I couldn't even do a single thing to protect what was mine.

And there was Kailyn . . .

The loss of her was devastating to me. I knew I hurt her with the words I threw at her. I knew I wasn't worthy of a chosen mate for her. With her being so far away from me, the bond was weakening. I could barely feel her now too.

Emptiness.

Total Emptiness.

That was all I felt. I was as hollow as can be. I threw the covers off of me and walked padded over to my phone. I picked it up and looked at the screen. I stared at it for what seems like an eternity as I fought an internal battle inside of me.

Was it better to just let them go?

What was the use of chasing something I have already lost?

I sat the phone back down with a decision that would change my life. I was going to let them go. They deserve better than someone like me. I glanced at the phone again and this time I picked it back up and threw it across the room. The phone shattered instantly as it hit the wall. Bits and pieces were falling to the ground.

My knees wobbled, and I fell onto my knees as I clutched at my chest. I hope she was happy. That was all I wanted if I couldn't have her.

*   *   *

TITUS

I woke up with Patience's naked body wrapped around me. What happened last night brought her and my bond a little closer. I could feel her wolf faintly in the back of my mind. A thin barrier only separated us. She sighed and snuggled closer. Her face was moving to the crook of my neck where she inhaled deeply.

"Yummy," she mumbled in her sleep.

"What is yummy?" I asked.

She sighed and intertwined her legs with mine. "You are, silly."

"How yummy? Yummy enough to go another round?" I asked. I felt her sigh and then stiffened. Her body was completely rigid as consciousness finally came. Slowly she pulled back and looked up at me. A blush formed on her cheeks as she realized just how skin to skin we are. She began pulling back but I tightened my arms around her. She turned to me with a pout.

I chuckled as I moved to kiss her lips. She responded instantly, her tongue shyly coming out to play with mine as we tasted each other. Something inside of me stirred and my heart swell up inside of me.

When she broke the kiss, her eyes were glimmering with desire and lust. It was hot and all I wanted to do was take her again. Many emotions ran through my body.

She was almost mine and all I had to do now was mark her. This will break the bond between our destined mates—freeing them and us from our bonds.

Patience adjusted her position. She was now sitting up with our blanket wrapped around her chest. Her dark brown hair was a mess on her head, and I couldn't help but grin. She looked adorable and sexy. I sat up next to her and kissed her shoulder. She turned slightly to look at me. I smoothed back her hair from her neck and kissed the place where I was going to mark her. She shivered and leaned into my body.

"Titus," she whispered. I hummed my answer and she tilted her head to give me better access. I trailed kisses up her neck to the back of her ear. "We should really get going."

My hand snaked around her front and pulled her closer to me.

"Tell me, when did you decide to start learning French?" I asked her. I saw her eyebrows come together and she turned slightly to look at me.

"If I am going to be staying here, I should be learning French. It is a language that a lot of people use here." She stated.

"Who taught you?" I asked.

She blush a little. "I did a little bit of researching here and there while I had time to myself. I hope I said it correctly."

She looked a little uncertain and immediately, I wanted to take that away. My fingers went to her chin and turned her towards me. I placed a quick kiss onto her lips.

"You did wonderful. If you want I can help you learn." I offered and her eyes lit up. That was much better. I couldn't help it but kissed her again. *"J'ai envie de toi."*

Her lips pursed again. "What did you just say?"

I smirked and shrugged. Getting up, I slipped on my boxer. "You will have to figure it out. Once you do, I will give you your award and your next lesson."

"What? Wait. Say it again." She quickly struggled to get out of bed with the blanket wrapped around her. I repeated what I said earlier and she stared at me with a blank face. I laughed at her reaction before turning into the bathroom. I heard her mumbling something about learning French and how a pain in the ass it was before I closed the door.

*　　　*　　　*

PATIENCE

I glared at the door as he disappeared behind it. I repeated what he said in my head and made a point in asking around to see if someone will tell me what it was. I peeked again at the door and noticed he was not out yet. I slipped the blanket off and pulled on a t-shirt and a pair of yoga shorts. I walked out of the bedroom and down the stairs to go find Kailyn.

I found her sitting with Christian and Emily on the breakfast table. They all looked up when they saw me. I walked over and sat next to Kailyn.

"Good morning." Kailyn leaned in and whispered. "I just wanted to tell you that Micah and I had to go back to his territory."

She scooted closer to me. "Do you think what I am doing is right? I feel guilty and sadness. Goddess, Patience, I feel so much emotions."

"What does your heart tell you?" I asked.

"To go bu—"

"Then go," I replied easily. "I felt the same way when I first found out about Kyle. I waited for so many years deciding if I should just move on or wait. It takes a lot of guts to do what you believe is right. If you believe this is what you want then go."

"I am not selfish?" she asked.

"Never, Kailyn," I said instantly. She nodded feeling slightly satisfied with my answer before eating again.

I turned to look at Christian. "What does *J'ai envie de toi* mean?"

Christian and Emily broke into grins as soon as I said it before they shook their head. "Figure it out on your own."

I pouted but at the corner of my eyes I caught movement. I turned to see a male staring right at me. He was staring at me boldly and it kind of unnerved me. I wondered who he was. I turned back to the group.

"Who is that male over there?" I pointed to the empty area. Christian turned to look but saw no one. He turned back to me looking confused.

"Who?"

"Where did he go?" I asked as I looked around the room again. He was nowhere to be found. It must've been my imagination."Never mind."

Titus came down shortly after and walked over to me. He leaned down to my ear and whispered. "Did you find out yet?"

"No," I replied while pursing my lips. Learning French was difficult. "I'm going to the library later."

CHAPTER 26

PATIENCE

I stared at the French to English translation book, and so far, I got nothing. I huffed and flipped a few more pages before I slammed it shut and pinched the bridge of my nose. It was giving me a headache. I moved a little on the couch until I was comfortably nestled into the plush cushion.

"If I couldn't translate a phrase through a book, I would need to get myself an instructor—someone besides him," I mumbled to myself. It was late, and I told no one to bother me, determined to figure out what the phrase was.

Just a nap and I would begin again where I started. I just needed to rest my mind just for a moment. A good rest would clear my mind. I could feel my body giving in and my muscles relaxing as my eyes fluttered close. I exhaled slowly, and soon, the comfortable darkness took over.

I awoke when I felt myself being pushed down. Instantly, my eyes opened to see the male from breakfast this morning hovering and staring down at me. I inched back as far as I could.

"Who are you?" I asked.

"It doesn't matter who I am." His eyes glinted with desires. His nose flared with lust. "You are truly beautiful like what they have been saying."

"Yes. Well, I am not yours. Now, leave me alone." I tried to push him off, but his grip on the couch tightened. He had me trapped between the sofa and him.

His free hand came to cup my cheek before moving lower to expose my neck. An evil grin came on his face. "You are no one's. That means you are free to claim."

"Touch me, and you're dead," I threatened as I felt a new anger course through me. He chuckled sarcastically before licking his lip.

"I always like a good fight. Now, be a good kitty and let me taste you." His face moved closer to mine, and I let out a warning growl. I saw his chapped lips curl into a smile.

When he was close enough, I head-butted him. He was taken aback for a moment before he growled and pinned me down on the couch, his weight completely on top of mine. I could feel his arousal against my stomach and bile rose up in my throat.

"Bitch, well then, if you won't play nice, I don't mind playing rough," he growled out as his lips crashed down on mine. His tongue was licking my lips, trying to force his way into my mouth.

I struggled and thrashed against him, trying to get him off me. My heart was beating so fast; I had never felt it move at this rate before. It was fear. I was scared for what he was going to do. It disgusted me.

"You and Amelia are two complete opposites. She came willingly to my bed. You, on the other hand, will be a lot harder to claim."

The male's hand came up to my side towards my breast, and I grabbed onto his hand to get him to stop. Surprisingly, the male's weight was completely lifted off me seconds later. I turned to see Titus's cold eyes looking at me. It held no warmth—only fury. It made me flinch as his eyes were looking at me accusingly. He turned towards the male with a predatory look. His skin was already prickling with hair.

133

The male scrambled to get up, but Titus was faster than he was. His hand came to the male's throat and squeezed tightly.

"She's mine!" Titus growled, and I heard the male gurgle as his air circulation was cut off.

"She's not marked, and she was willing to let me kiss and fuck her." The male taunted, and a roar escaped Titus's lips.

His hands were coming up to swipe at Titus's chest in weak attempts to free him. In one swift movement, Titus ripped the male's throat with no mercy.

The male's body fell to the ground, lifeless and dead. When Titus turned to look at me, his eyes still looked at me with accusations.

"Titus, let me explain."

"That's what she exactly said when I caught her," Titus growled out angrily, and in a flash, he was in front of me. His hand came around my neck, gripping it tightly that I let out a whimper of pain.

"Titus, please," I whispered trying to calm him, but I only saw black pools of darkness. His anger was beyond control.

"He was on top of you! Don't deny what I saw." He accused me angrily.

"No! He—"

His grip on my neck tightened even more, and I tried to remove his grip from me.

"Let me go! You are hurting me!" I growled out.

"No!" he roared back. "You *will* listen. You are mine. You are not to be near any other males!"

"Titus, let me go, or I swear to goddess I will fucking run away from you." I tugged on his arm harder.

"You will not run away from me, and I will make sure of it," he roared before his canine elongated and came at my throat. I did not want this. No. I did not want him to mark me out of anger. Completing the mating process should be something consensual. I was about to say something, but I felt it. I felt the moment his teeth

134

pierced my skin. I felt the moment his canine sunk in completely, and I felt the moment my soul combined with his.

I pounded and slapped on his chest to get him to stop. I knew he felt what I felt but only stronger. He now had the presence of my soul and my wolf in his mind. I heard him inhale sharply before releasing my neck. He took a step back.

I saw blood dripping down his mouth and chin. I clutched at my neck from the mark he made. Tears welled up in my eyes, and I shook my head. He looked guilty.

"Patience," he was the first to talk.

"No," I said. "You don't get to talk. I do. How could you do this? Are you happy now? Do you feel what I felt what the male did to me earlier? Do you see that I was telling the truth? I understand you were hurt, but you should remember that I was too."

"Patience." His hands came out to grab for me, but I took a step back.

"No," I repeated. "Don't. You don't get to do this. I can't believe you, Titus. You let your animal take over. You wouldn't even listen to me. J-Just don't."

I moved around him and darted out of the room. Tears were streaming down my cheeks as I ran as fast as I could to the bedroom. When I got inside, I slammed the door close and ran to the bathroom. I moved to take a shower and scrub my body from everything.

I felt pain in my chest, and I clutched at it. The bond with Kyle was living on a thread as the bond with Titus intensified. I knew Titus could feel what I was feeling. I was feeling betrayed and hurt.

I pulled on one of his t-shirts and crawled into bed where I pulled my knees up to my chest as I cried.

*　　　*　　　*

TITUS

I stood outside our bedroom door, and I could hear Patience's soft cries from the other side. My hand came out to touch the door, wishing it was her who I was touching. I didn't know why I did that. I was so blinded by anger and jealousy. I forgot she was not Amelia. I marked Patience unwillingly.

I could feel her presence in my mind. Her emotions could be read like a book. Her heart could be heard from miles away. She was there with me, and she was beautiful. Her heart was pure and gentle.

I had hurt her.

I had betrayed her.

I did the weakest and most shameful thing a werewolf could do.

But...

I couldn't leave her. I was crazily drawn to her. It was unexplainable that I found myself standing here. I placed my forehead against the cold door and exhaled as I closed my eyes. The need to be next to her was strong. The marking was still so new and fresh. My wolf and I both needed to be next to her. It was a way of marking. It was a bond that was only halfway created and the bond needed to feel complete. I was lost without her, even if she was on the other side of the door.

I could only hope she would forgive me.

The look I saw on her face in the library killed me inside, and if she ever forgave me, I would make sure she never looked at me that way again. I felt a stab of pain in my chest, and I knew it was her pain mixed with mine. She was hurting.

I inaudibly whispered her name as I heard her crying slowing down.

I didn't know how long I stood outside the door, waiting and listening to her, but when there was nothing but silence, I opened the door slowly to see her sleeping on top of the covers curled up in a fetal position. My feet started moving, and soon, I was next to the bed. I sat down as I lifted my hand to smooth back her hair. Her cheeks were wet with tears.

The amount of guilt I felt was torturous. I realized just how much I didn't want to see her hurt. To know that it was me who put it there was killing me inside.

Slowly, I lifted her body and placed her under the cover. I was happy that even though she was angry with me, she still found comfort in my scent as she had on my shirt. After I tucked her in, I slipped in behind her and pulled her close. I knew she would probably be angry in the morning, but I needed her close. It soothed both of our wolves.

She turned in her sleep and snuggled closer to me. Her face was in the crook of my neck and her leg in between mine.

*   *   *

KAILYN

I needed to do this.

I stared at the phone for a moment before I started dialing. It was late, and Micah was asleep. I snuck my way into Alpha Titus's office with one intention on my mind.

When someone picked up on the other line, it was a voice that no longer had an effect on me, but it still brought back a nostalgic feeling. We went around life the wrong way and in turn, hurt all of us.

"Kyle?" I asked.

"Kailyn?" he sounded surprised.

"Yes, it is me," I replied sadly.

There was a moment of silence before I spoke up again.

"I want to say—"

"I am sorry."

We both began at once, and then we both gave a sad laugh before I spoke up again, "You go first."

"I am sorry, Kailyn. I didn't mean to hurt you. I know this is all messed up, and I know we can never fix what we have even if we wanted to. I just wanted to let you know I did love you. I loved you so much, Kailyn. I just wasn't strong enough to resist the bond I had with your sister, and the longer we were together, the harder it was," Kyle spoke sadly. "I never wanted to hurt you."

"I know," I replied. "I am sorry too, Kyle. I can't come back. There is a reason why I called you."

I paused for a moment to inhale slowly. "I found my mate."

There was a brief moment when I didn't hear him respond until he sighed and then spoke, "I am happy for you, Kailyn. Take it. Don't do what I did. Moon Goddess made him for you. He is yours."

"Thank you," I spoke softly.

"It's okay, Kailyn. If you think about it, I can go all big bad wolf and go in a jealous rampage using my animalistic need to come over there and kill the male who took what was mine or I can be the better person than my wolf and let go. It is the hardest thing ever, Kailyn. The urge to come there is overwhelming. Every day I would talk myself out of it. The bond that I have with you is disappearing," he replied gently. I heard his sharp breathing as he sighed.

"You will find someone for you, Kyle," I whispered back. He was nothing more than a friend now. It felt weird, but it also was a comfortable atmosphere.

"I think I am going to focus on myself for now. I am sorry, Kailyn. I wish things were different. Just remember that even though you and I are no longer together, you will always find safety here. I will always protect you. You will always be my friend," he said, and a tear slipped from my eyes.

"You will always be mine," I replied hoarsely.

"I'll talk to you soon?" he whispered back, his voice also hoarse.

"Yes, definitely. Goodbye, Kyle," I said before hanging up. My emotions were all over, but one thing I knew was that I did the right thing. Kyle and I would always be friends, and it would never be anything more.

CHAPTER 27

PATIENCE

I woke up the next morning with my body humming all over with a tingling sensation. Right away, I knew who it was. My heart was calm, and my breathing was regular. I could feel my wolf purring with satisfaction.

Titus.

He must've come to bed last night after I fell asleep. I moved a little to get away from him, but he held on tight. Lifting my head, I glanced up to see he was wide awake and looking down at me with those intense icy blue eyes that tugged on my heartstrings. He held nothing back. His facial expression told me he was regretting everything.

I wasn't sure exactly how I was feeling right now. At this very moment, my wolf was content, but a part of me was still furious with him. I was hurt, and I didn't want to give in easily. I looked away from him. It was getting too hard. My resistance was slipping away as I looked upon his beautiful face.

I knew he could feel every single emotion I was feeling. His sharp intake told me he felt the hurt, but he also felt the happiness I had as well. His hand came out to cup my cheek, bringing me back to look at him.

"I am sorry. I know that it doesn't change anything, but I really am. I wish I could change things. I was in a rage. When I saw that male on top of you, my mind flashed back to Amelia. Only it was more painful with you. All I saw was red, and I didn't stop to think." His finger rubbed my cheeks. I closed my eyes at the touch. It was soft and comforting. "You deserve someone better. I hate Kyle and the fact that he hurt you, but now, I am just like him. I hate myself for doing that to you."

"Stop." The word left my mouth before I could even comprehend what happened.

Something shattered in his eyes, and his facial expression slipped. He was now hurt as well.

Damn it.

No, Titus.

I want to be mad at you.

I closed my eyes again to stop myself from giving in, but I knew deep inside I had forgiven him already. He was mine as much as I was his. There was no reason to avoid it.

Although he went about it the wrong way, he had never hurt me in the past.

"Tell me what I have to do for you to forgive me, Patience," his voice sounded tortured as if I had just starved him for days without water. "I can't live like this, knowing you hate me. *Je ne peux pas vivre sans toi. S'il vous plait, j'ai besoin de toi.* (I can't live without you. Please, I need you.)"

His French weaved its way into my heart. It sounded so broken, so lost, even when I couldn't understand it. I could feel it in his voice. My instinct told me to soothe him. My wolf was howling in sadness because I refused to.

"Titus," I spoke, exhaling in the process. "You hurt me."

"I know," his voice cracked. His breathing was harsh and short as if he was gasping for air. I swallowed hard, refusing to look at him. "It's killing me, Patience."

My hand came up to caress his chest gently. His breathing slowed down and became deeper.

"What did you say?" I asked suddenly, wondering what he said in French.

"I can't live without you. Please, I need you," he said hoarsely back, and his arms tightened around me. "I need you in my life in order to be able to survive it. Please forgive me, Patience. I would crawl on my knees for you to see how sorry I am."

My heart twisted, and the last of my resistance left me. I let go of the stiffness in my back and snuggled closer to his body. I inhaled his scent that I adored so much. It calmed my soul that was now intertwined with his.

"Patience, you can do anything to me. Please, you can beat me up, hit me, slap me . . . Hell, you can even mark me. I don't care. Please just forgive me," he begged again after I didn't respond.

I gave a small soft laugh before opening my eyes to look up at him. He looked at me with wide eyes, a little surprised at my laugh.

"Then let me mark you, my alpha," I whispered. For a moment, he was stunned before his eyes darkened lustfully and his lips curled into a smile.

He moved us so that I was now straddling his hips and he was sitting up. I moved my hands to cup his cheeks. He tilted his head to the side to allow me better access. I licked my lips in anticipation, and a rumbling stirred in his chest in response. I glanced briefly back at him and saw how he was looking at me. The ache in between my legs increased. Arousal was oozing from me, and I knew he could smell me. His hands rested on my hips.

I moved in.

My lips met his neck, and a seductive growl came from his lips. I grinned slightly before nibbling my way around his neck. He groaned and tightened his grip on my hips. His fingers were digging into my hips as he was fighting for control.

When I found what I was looking for, my canine elongated. I ran it along his skin.

"Patience," he barked.

I giggled before I dug my canine into his neck where his pulse beat. His grip on my hips tightened even more. The moment I dug in, I felt everything about him.

His wolf.

His soul.

His heart.

His heart was beating so fast. His soul and wolf were strong and fierce. They were two dominant souls combined into one. I could feel the pride he had for me. I could feel the desires and lust he was feeling. He loved how I marked him. It aroused him like nothing else.

The glow of our bond shined brighter than anything else, and what was left of my bond with Kyle immediately disappeared. My heart began beating as one with Titus. He was now mine.

When I was done, I licked his wound clean before licking my lips. I pulled back to look at him, and his eyes held so much emotion. One of his hands came out to cup me behind my neck before pulling me down for a kiss. His eyelids were dropping slowly as my lips came closer to his. The moment our lips met, I closed my eyes at the sheer bliss that pulsed through my body.

I had never experienced anything like it.

It was like drinking water for the first time after days of walking in the desert.

His grip tightened behind my neck, and the kiss deepened. An animalistic growl came from him, and it only aroused me more. We kissed like we had been starved. His tongue licked and sucked mine until we were both fighting for dominance. Finally, we broke the kiss, both panting at the effect the kiss had on us.

"Mine," he whispered against my lips before giving me a quick kiss again.

"Mine," I whispered back and nipped his lower lip. A slow smirk made onto his face.

"Yours," he replied, and an animalistic possessive growl came from me. I slapped my hand over my mouth. He chuckled at my reaction.

I slapped him playfully. "I am not usually like this."

"Your wolf is. You like it when I say I am yours, *ma cherie*?" he teased as he came back in for another kiss.

I did. I liked it so much. It was such a turn-on. When he pulled back, his finger came out to touch my swollen lips.

"Thank you for forgiving me."

"I would've made you suffer longer . . ." I began.

"No, you wouldn't have," he simply stated. "You care for me."

He was prodding in my mind. I pursed my lips and pinched him. "Stop reading my emotions."

"You do, though, don't you?" he asked.

I looked at him and saw he was slightly uncertain. "I do."

He gave me a smirk before his confidence was restored. I don't know how he managed it, but before I could even say anything, he had us off the bed, my legs wrapped around his waist. He carried me into the bathroom.

"Where are we going?" I eyed him suspiciously.

He leaned in to nibble on my jawline before kissing the mark on my neck. "Taking a shower together."

Wait, what?

*   *   *

NOOR

Everyone seemed to have found their mate. I couldn't help but feel a stab of jealousy towards Christian and Titus. They got to feel the bond of their soulmate. Growling in irritation, I worked my body vigorously against the punching bag in the gym. My hands landed hard blows, making dust swarm in the air.

The sweat beaded down my forehead and to my chin. My muscles ached from all the work, but I kept at it. I was so concentrated on punching it. I didn't hear Christian walk in. He clapped his hands and walked over to sit on the bench press. He placed his elbows on his knees as he watched me.

"What do you want?" I asked as I wiped sweat from my forehead.

"Why are you working yourself so hard?" he asked.

"Because I don't have a mate to keep me in bed," I retorted. Christian chuckled before standing up. He walked up and sent a punch to my side. I growled and turned to punch him in the face. He fell to the ground but then tripped me with his legs. I fell hard onto my knees. I saw his hand come back up for another hard punch, but I rolled away.

"Why are you so bitter?" Christian taunted.

"Fuck you, Christian," I muttered as I stood up. He followed suit and rubbed his chin.

"Your time will come." Christian looked at me with encouragement. He moved to tap my back with his hand.

"Not fast enough, man," I replied. "You got lucky with yours. She dropped right into your lap."

Christian grinned then. His eyes were briefly distant as he thought about his mate. The mark on his neck was fresh.

"You know, now that Titus has his mate, he is more than willing to let you go out to go find her," Christian said as he moved to grab a towel and toss it at me.

I grabbed it mid-air and wiped my sweat from my forehead to my back and down my chest. I wrapped the towel around my neck as I picked up my water bottle to take a long gulp.

"I was thinking about it, but I wasn't sure how to approach Titus. He has been so busy."

"Did you feel it?" Christian asked, and I knew what he meant.

"Our alpha finally completed the mating process." I confirmed with Christian. We were both grinning as we felt the bond with our luna grow stronger.

Christian patted me again on the back before we walked out of the gym together.

Christian was right. It was my time to go and find my mate. If she wasn't going to find me, I had to look for her. A smile came on my face as I thought about the many things I would do when I see her.

With a new mission on my mind, I quickly headed to my bedroom to shower and pack. After that, I was going to talk to Titus and leave in search of my mate.

CHAPTER 28

PATIENCE

Titus insisted that I wore my hair up today. I guessed he thought I didn't know what he was thinking, but I was almost positive the possessive and dominating male wanted everyone to see his mark on my neck. I clenched my core, and I literally had to tear myself away from him in order to escape the bedroom.

When I made it downstairs, I saw that Christian and Noor were heading out from behind the stairs. They were quietly talking until they heard me. Christian was grinning, and Noor looked a little nervous.

"Where is the alpha?" Christian asked.

"Upstairs," I responded. "Did you two just come back from training?"

"I needed a workout," Noor responded.

"I think you should wake Titus up for training every morning," I replied.

Christian and Noor laughed, and I shrugged. "It's the truth. The male has a drive that is insatiable."

Kailyn came bounding down the stairs. Her eyes were looking at me, and I knew exactly what she needed. She grabbed my arm and pulled me away from the guys. I waved them goodbye before heading out the door with Kailyn. We ran to our sitting spot from yesterday where she made me sit as she began pacing.

"What happened? Was it Micah? Did he do something? Do I need to kill him?" I stood up and was about to head back inside when Kailyn pulled me back.

"I spoke to Kyle."

I went quiet. She saw my reaction and rushed to explain herself.

"I only called him to tell him that I wasn't coming back and that I met my mate," she said. "H-He was happy for me."

"He was?" I was surprised.

"Yes. I expected him to flip, but then everything kind of just settled. He was okay with everything. He understood and told me to go with Micah." She began.

This was very interesting. Was Kyle really letting Kailyn go? And if he did, what was his intention behind it? Was he going to come after me? I hoped not because I knew he felt the marking. I felt bad for him in a way, but I knew he deserved it.

The reason why my bond with Kyle still existed even after he mated with Kailyn was that he never really let me go. In my case, I let him go. In my heart, there was no more Kyle. The bond broke easier for us when I did that.

Kailyn pointed at my neck. "It looks like you are fully mated."

I touched it, and a tingling went through my body. "I did."

"How do you feel?" she asked with curiosity.

"I can feel him, his presence in my mind at all times. When he feels I am anxious, he sends me reassurance. When I felt his anger, I could feel my wolf trying to calm him down. It is weird to have someone in your head at all times, but it is like we are one," I said.

"Am I going to feel that way with Micah?" she asked. "Would it be different from Kyle's? I can already feel Micah. My mark on him is strong, Patience. Would it be different?"

I shrugged because I honestly didn't know the answer. "Have you decided to go with Micah then?"

She nodded. "Kyle and I are just friends now. Besides, I don't think Micah will let me leave. I have to face fate as it was given to me. I understand what Kyle meant when he said the bond was too strong. I can see why he went crazy when you left him. Honestly, I don't know if I can't hate him that long. A person only does what he or she thought was right. We don't know for right away if it is wrong."

She paused for a moment before she moved to sit down next to me. She grabbed my hand and pulled into her lap as she placed her other hand on top of mine.

"Patience, I am going home with Micah today. He had asked me to go. I am nervous about leaving you and my past behind. This is a huge step for me. I feel like I haven't apologized enough, and I feel like I still need to be by your side." She began.

"Go. Be happy. I am fine here. I have a home. You have a mate. I forgive you," I responded to her and squeezed her hand. She smiled and wrapped her arms around me, and I did the same.

It was then we heard clapping behind us. It made us snap our heads back to take a startling look. Much to my displeasure, it was Amelia. She stood there with an insane grin. Her eyes were looking at us with a malicious vengeance.

"This is all very sweet," she spoke. "But I am afraid I am going to have to cut this short. The two of you have been nothing but trouble ever since you two have been here."

"Amelia, don't you have something to do?" I growled as I stood up. Her eyes lit up when I said that. She snapped her fingers, and four large males came out from the bushes, stalking towards us.

"Now that you mention it, yes. Yes, I do," she responded.

Kailyn and I looked at each other before she took down the nearest male. I moved to take the one who placed a hand on my shoulder. He dropped to the floor, and I kicked him in the throat. He doubled over in pain. The other one came charging at me and wrapped his arms around my torso, trapping my arms. I threw my head back and hit him square in the nose. The blood squirting got him yelping out in pain. Amelia growled.

"Imbeciles!" she muttered before coming after me.

She tried to throw a punch at my face, but I caught her fist in my hand, quickly twisting it. When I heard the sound of bones breaking, I knew I snapped her arm. She screamed before hitting me with her other hand. I blocked it before throwing a punch at her face. I had to admit: I enjoyed hitting her.

I was about to pin Amelia to the ground when I heard another male speak, "Stop."

I turned towards the voice to see Kailyn struggling in his grasp, a silver knife pointing straight at her heart. Immediately, I let go of Amelia. She stood up, clutching at her arm. She wiped away the blood from her lip, and I put my hands up.

"Let her go," I said.

The man laughed. "And have her go tell her mate and yours? No, thank you."

"Don't do something you might regret. My mate will kill you faster than you can blink." I threatened. Kailyn looked at me pleadingly.

"Come with us, and she won't die. You refuse, and you will see just how fast your sister will die," he retorted, and I snarled.

"Enough talking. We don't have time. Take them. We have to leave now." Amelia ordered. The males I took down stood up and walked to me, holding onto their injury. They tied me up with Kailyn next to me, and they took us away.

The pack house was fading from sight as we moved deeper into the woods. It didn't take long until we reached a dirt road where a black SUV was parked. They threw us both in and tied up Kailyn as well. Amelia moved in next to us while the two males went to sit in the front.

"Why are you doing this?" I asked her.

"That is for me to know and for you to find out." She took out a cloth and placed it on her lap as she spilled what I think was chloroform on it. The smell was intense. It did knock us out pretty quickly, and because we were werewolves, our bodies absorbed it quickly. I was guessing she wanted to knock us out long enough so that she could take us where she wanted to.

Amelia put the cloth on my face, but I struggled to get it away from me. She pulled it back and slapped me hard across the face. It was painful. I closed my eyes briefly before opening.

"Slap me again, and I swear I will kill you the second my hands are freed," I hoarsely spat.

She smirked and placed the cloth on my mouth this time. I struggled and tried not to breathe the content, only it didn't help much. I could also feel Kailyn struggling next to me, and soon, I became unconscious.

*   *   *

When I awoke, I was on a bed in a room with no windows. A light hung above me, but it was dim. I squinted around the room until my eyes adjusted. I saw that Kailyn was still unconscious next to me. I nudged her.

"Kailyn," I whispered. I nudged her again.

She slowly stirred before she opened her eyes and looked around. Her eyes adjusted to the dark before she looked at me.

"Where are we? What are we going to do?"

"I don't know. We need to find a way to free ourselves," I replied. I could feel Titus through the bond faintly. He and his wolf were on edge.

"We aren't going to be able to free ourselves. It is a melted silver rope." Kailyn tugged on it. I winced as I tugged it hard, but it was a wasted effort. The handcuffs were made specifically for werewolves. Silver weakened our wolves.

The door whipped open, and Amelia sauntered in. She had her arm wrapped up in a sling as she approached us. She sat on the edge of the bed and tilted her head slightly, a smirk appearing on her face.

"You're awake," she whispered.

"You're insane," I spat. She cackled and shook her head.

"Maybe you're right," she replied.

"Why are you doing this, Amelia? Let us go, and I will not tell Titus." I urged.

She laughed before glaring at me. "Are you really going to ask me that? I know what you two have been doing. I fucking felt it."

"He is not yours. He's mine," I responded, which earned me a punch in the face. I fell onto the bed. Kailyn screamed profanity at Amelia as my sister moved closer to me to protect me.

"You think you are all bad, beating us up like this. How about you let us go, and we will see who the stronger one is." Kailyn cut in. I could hear the anger in her voice.

Amelia gave Kailyn her maniac beam before she moved to a drawer and took out a silver carving knife. It was long, and at the very tip of it was curved enough to mark skin. It was a hunting knife.

"How about I show you just how strong I am?" She snickered.

She moved closer to us. "I was thinking about that pretty little face of yours, Patience."

She ran her knife along my cheek before I felt it dig into my skin. I cried out as tears leaked from my cheek. Kailyn cried out and tried to cover me. Amelia cackled and pulled back as she looked at Kailyn with renewed interest.

"Aww, you're so brave." She cooed before she leaned down and placed the carving knife on Kailyn's neck. "You're just a slut. Who do you think you are? You picked your chosen, and now, you're going to leave with Alpha Micah? I should just kill you. You

152

don't deserve happiness just like your sister. What made you two so special? Two mates in one life?"

I heard Kailyn scream as the knife dug into her neck; blood seeped from her wound. I struggled to help her, but I was helpless. Amelia had gone insane. I prayed and hoped that Titus was now looking for me.

CHAPTER 29

I felt dread crawling up in the pit of my stomach. My heart was beating rapidly, and my breathing became irregular. It was strange because I was only speaking to Noor in my office. I glanced around the room and found nothing out of the ordinary.

"What's wrong?" Noor suddenly stopped mid-sentence to ask me. My gaze flickered back to him.

"I'm not sure. I feel . . ." I frowned slightly. "I feel scared."

Noor's facial expression changed as soon as he realized what was happening, and once I saw the knowing look on his face, I knew it was about Patience. My heartbeat sped to a fearful height. Not wasting another second, I burst out of my chair and ran down the stairs. Christian was with Emily at the breakfast table. They were conversing casually back and forth until they saw me running like a madman.

"Where is your luna?" I asked Christian.

"Kailyn took her outside." Christian pointed to the door, and I immediately ran out. "Hey, wait, what's going on?"

I heard Noor's and Christian's footsteps close behind me before I was knocked to the ground by someone. I struggled to remove the body from me. It was difficult as the body on top of me was trying to throw a punch at me. I moved to block the blow.

Noor and Christian came up and moved the body off. It was Alpha Micah, and he looked just as crazy as I do.

"Where is Kailyn?" he asked. "You knew I was going to take her today. You are hiding her!"

"You're an idiot!" I growled out. Alpha Micah struggled in Noor and Christian's grasps.

"I'm going to kill you." Micah struggled even more.

"I don't have time to deal with you." I started walking away, but Micah was able to escape from their hold, and I went flying down to the ground again. I managed to flip Micah over and threw a punch at his face, dizzying him for a moment. The fool was going to make us lose what we had left to trace them.

"Where did you take her?" Micah asked again.

"Listen, and you listen very carefully because I would only repeat this once. My mate has disappeared. I can feel it in our bonds. Something has happened." I reasoned with him. Alpha Micah's struggled died down, and I could see fear reflecting in his eyes.

"Are you saying Kailyn is with her?" he asked.

"If you don't see her around and neither do I, I would assume she is with my mate," I replied and let him go. I moved to stand up and walked away from him. When he was released, he rubbed his arms before walking up to me.

"Where are they?" he asked.

"I was about to find out until you knocked me down." I turned to Noor and Christian. "Go and check if anyone is missing."

As soon as Noor and Christian were out of sight, Alpha Micah and I jogged down to the place where our mates hung out. Their faint scents lingered in the air along with one that I recognized and a few others I knew were rogues.

"Who was here with them?" Alpha Micah turned to look at me as soon as he sniffed what I smelled.

"Amelia," I whispered. Dread ran through my veins, and I felt like a rug had slipped out from under me. Amelia had Patience. Alpha Micah's eyes narrowed at me.

"Your destined mate did this? She kidnapped my mate and yours?" he asked.

"Don't," I started before breaking into a jog to follow the scent. I didn't want to start with Amelia because it would only stir whatever anger I had for her, and I needed to focus on finding Patience first. After, I would mercilessly end Amelia's life. She better not touch a single hair on Patience.

When we got to where their scents stopped, I looked down at the ground and saw tire tracks. After inspecting it carefully, I stood back up and turned to Alpha Micah.

"They went by vehicle. We will have to follow the tire tracks. My beta and gamma will be able to follow us by our scents. I can't wait any longer. I need to find her," I said as I began moving.

"I am not going to argue with you on that," Alpha Micah muttered before breaking into a jog next to me. We followed the tire tracks to an old warehouse an hour from my pack house. I didn't recognize who it was, but as soon as I saw a car nearby, I knew we had found them.

We evaluated our surroundings first to see if there was an easy way in. Unfortunately, the warehouse was a small one and only had one way in and one way out. We moved with caution closer to the door, and I raised up a hand to stop Alpha Micah from opening as I leaned against it.

When I heard no movements on the other side, I nodded as he opened the door. After entering, our eyes quickly adjusted to the dark, and we walked deeper into the warehouse. A chilling scream sent a bad shiver through my spine. I could see the look of panic on Micah's face as he recognized the voice.

His heart spoke for his mind now, and he moved towards the sound without thinking. I grabbed his elbow to stop him from going. We needed a plan, and he wasn't thinking. Another scream came, and this one was different. This one tore at my heart.

Patience.

"We need to get to them! Who knows what that crazy destined mate of yours is doing to her?" Micah angrily whispered.

"We need a plan. We can't go marching in there. Who knows what they have?" I asked. "Calm down, Alpha Micah, and think."

"A plan? My plan is to kill that destined mate of yours. I am going to skin her alive and rip her throat," Alpha Micah growled.

"Okay, how are you going to do that? Are you going to just enter and say, 'Hey, I'm going to kill you?'" I grounded out.

"She's hurting them, you mutt!" Alpha Micah replied, and I shook my head. I knew Amelia was hurting them, but we couldn't be irrational. Not when it came to our mates' lives. I was about to answer him, but something stopped me.

Out of the corner of my eyes, I saw movements. I turned to look and saw that it was a big rogue. He grinned as he came closer. I saw another one coming from the opposite end. Alpha Micah also noticed them the same time I did.

With our backs turned to each other, we faced our opponents. When they charged at us, Alpha Micah and I pulled apart. His attention now rested on the other rogue as I maneuvered myself so that the rogue I was fighting with was sent to the ground. He muttered a curse as he got up and came at me again. I ducked under his fist and threw a hard punch at his stomach. I took out all my frustration on him. He was wasting my time, and I needed to get to Patience.

He was hurled to the ground, clutching at his stomach. From the corner of my eyes, Alpha Micah was casted to a few boxes before he stood up and sent the rogue to the opposite direction.

Suddenly, my opponent twisted his legs between mine. I lost my balance and stumbled to the ground. He crawled over my body and began punching at me. The blows were hard, and I could feel each hit, but it was weak and predictable for me. I managed to block his blows before I found an escape and threw his body off from mine. I stood up to finish the job when I felt something sting my back. I turned around to see another rogue with a tranquilizer in his hand, staring at me with a grin.

Fuck. I got taken down by a tranquilizer gun. This is one story not to tell the pups we will have if Patience and I ever leave this godforsaken place.

I struggled to stay awake, but my vision began blurring even when I fought it using all the strength that I had. The tranquilizer was enough to put a big horse to sleep. I staggered to get away. It was useless, and I was going down. I regret not finishing the job earlier with the rogue I was fighting with. I should've been more aware of my surroundings, but I was too consumed by my anger. Patience was the last thought on my mind before darkness took over my vision, and I lost consciousness.

When I awoke, I was in a room and tied to a metal chair with silver chains. I blinked a couple of times before lifting my head to look around. I saw Alpha Micah first; he was seated next to me, also handcuffed in silver chains. He was awake, and his eyes were looking ahead. I turned to see Patience and Kailyn riddled with wounds on their faces and necks. Blood was dripping from their wounds as tears ran down their cheeks.

"Patience." I began struggling to get out of the chains, but the enemies made sure I couldn't get out. It didn't stop me though. I continued to struggle until a whimper escaped Patience's lips.

"Don't," she weakly spoke. "It's useless."

"I'm sorry," I whispered.

She gave a small short laugh. "I should've killed Amelia the moment I had the chance, but I wanted everyone to like me."

Her gaze darted back up to look at me and then at Alpha Micah. "You two were supposed to rescue us, not get captured with us."

"Is she okay?" Alpha Micah asked hoarsely as his eyes remained on Kailyn's unconscious form.

Patience glanced down at Kailyn who was sleeping on her lap. "She's fine. Amelia did a number on her. She is losing a lot of blood."

Alpha Micah growled as he looked at his mate. I exactly knew what he was feeling. Our mates were so close to us, yet we couldn't touch them. We couldn't save them. They were hurt. The one thing that meant the world to us were in pain, and we couldn't protect them.

"After this is over, I will never go into the woods again," Patience muttered. The corner of my lips lifted. Even after getting injured, she was still positive, and I silently promised I would do everything I could for her to be alive.

"After this is over, you will be locked in our room forever," I replied. Alpha Micah made a noise of agreement.

"Well, we don't need to go to that extreme," she reasoned slowly. "It wasn't like I was running away or I wasn't on your land. I was on your land, which, I might add, should've been safe."

"I will have to agree with her on that," Alpha Micah replied. I threw him a glare, and he managed a shrug. "Four rogues managed to enter your land and kidnapped your luna and mine. You need to tighten your security."

I growled. "We are not talking about this right now. We need to figure a way out."

"Kailyn and I tried, but our handcuffs are made out of silver," she said.

I looked around, and so did Alpha Micah. We were located in the middle of the room. There was no chance of us getting anywhere close to grabbing something to help free us. I refused to give up as I thought over what else we could do, but I was interrupted when the door to the room opened and revealed Amelia. She smiled when she saw that we were awake.

"And the two sleeping alphas are awake." She walked over to her table where she picked up a carving knife. She examined it carefully before walking over to pull a chair in front of me. She sat down and crossed her legs, placing her hand and knife into her lap as she looked at me.

"Amelia, I am warning you to stop what you are doing." I ordered.

She giggled. "Oh, don't you start, Titus. I am the one with the upper hand here, not you. Now, be a nice little mutt, and I won't hurt your precious Patience that much. One wrong move from you, and I can and will end her life in front of your eyes."

I growled as I struggled out of the tightening chains. My wolf wanted to kill the person who just threatened what was his. Alpha Micah began struggling, and Amelia's happy eyes moved towards him.

"I almost forgot about you." She stood up and moved in front of Alpha Micah where she leaned down and traced the knife on his cheek. "I had fun with

Kailyn. I made sure to cut her old mark. It looks a little dirty, but I am sure it will look even more hideous after."

"Bitch!" Alpha Micah roared as he struggled even harder.

She laughed and stepped away as she walked over to sit on the edge of the bed next to Patience. The air seemed to have grown thinner, and I was finding it harder to breathe. I stared carefully at Amelia. I knew my options were low.

"What do you want?" I asked.

"I want to end all of you." She turned to look at me again, her vengeful eyes flaring up with rage. "You could've forgiven me. I could've been luna. We could've been happy. She wouldn't have been in our life then."

"You want me? You want the luna position?" I repeated her points out. It was fucking hilarious that she thought I would take her back. It wasn't going to happen. It would never happen.

"Yes! We could go back to what we used to be!" she stated as her body stiffened in rage.

"Let her go, and you and I will talk," I said as I glanced at Patience.

She giggled. "Oh, I am not that stupid, Titus. You think I am. You kept me in your pack, and you treated me like an idiot. You thought I would just forget you and find myself another mate? You parade your new luna in front of my eyes. You even mated her completely. You are stupid to think that I am, and for that, I will show you just how stupid you are."

She stood up and turned towards Patience. Patience shook her head as she knew what was coming. Amelia lifted the knife into the air and was about to put another mark on Patience's soft skin when we heard a commotion outside. Amelia turned towards the noise, and she dropped her hands.

"I will be back," she replied before setting her knife down on the table and walking out of the room.

CHAPTER 30

PATIENCE

As soon as Amelia left, I let out the breath I was holding. I didn't know how much longer I could take the pain. I could feel every inch of my cheeks down to my neck, every cut she made. I glanced down to see that Kailyn was slowly stirring.

"Kailyn," Alpha Micah also noticed.

Kailyn's eyes fluttered open, and I could see reality set in as she began whimpering. She also had cuts riddling her cheeks and neck. She slowly pushed herself off me.

"Kailyn," Alpha Micah's voice was hoarse as tears ran down his cheeks.

Her eyes found him and tears began rolling down her cheeks, but because of the saltiness of her tears, it burned her cheeks. She let out a small cry of pain. Alpha Micah struggled harder as he could see her in pain.

"Are you okay?" he asked. "Talk to me, please."

She nodded and tried to stop her crying. "I am fine. How did you two get here?"

"Apparently, they were our rescue party," I muttered.

Titus threw me a glare. Kailyn frowned as she looked at them.

"I'm guessing they failed, as they are now tied up just like us," Kailyn replied. Alpha Micah growled out.

The noise grew louder; we heard shouting and crashing. When the door flew open, I was relieved to see it was Noor. He glanced around the room and immediately came to us. He grabbed our wrists and looked at our ankles and began looking around the room for the key.

"About time," Titus murmured. "Hurry up and free us."

"That is what I am about to do, but where the hell is the key?" he asked, and when he couldn't find it he swore under his breath before grabbing an axe. "Keep your hands apart."

He walked over to me, and I spread my wrist apart from each other as far as possible. I heard the swish motion of the axe before it came down on the silver. It broke in two. I moved to untie my feet. He moved to Kailyn next. After I was done, I moved quickly to Titus where I grabbed his cheek to examine him. He closed his eyes at my touch before opening them to look at me.

"You need to leave. We can take care of this," Titus said, and I shook my head. He rolled his eyes. "Why am I not surprised you will say no?"

Kailyn was freed, and Noor came over to break the chain from Alpha Micah before moving to Titus. Once freed, Alpha Micah pulled Kailyn into his arms. Titus came up to me and touched my face gently. I winced in pain.

"I'm going to kill her."

"Not if I get to her first," I muttered before turning around to head out the door, but Titus grabbed my elbow and held me back.

"Be reasonable, Patience," he said, and I glared at him.

"Nobody hurts my sister or me and gets away with it. Titus, either you let me do what I want to do, or I will do it without you," I demanded as I turned to look at him. He sighed and waved his hand for Alpha Micah to take Kailyn and leave first. Alpha Micah hesitated as I could see he also wanted to fight, but Kailyn was crying, and he knew she was his priority. He nodded and headed out the door quickly.

Noor came up beside us. "Christian is currently holding off four rogues. I think we should go and help him out."

Titus nodded and allowed Noor to lead us out the door. When we arrived upon the scene, Christian was just being knocked down to the ground with a kick behind the knee. Noor quickly jumped in and began shoving the rogues off Christian. Titus turned to me and held onto my arms.

"Stay here," He ordered before turning to go and help his beta and gamma. I wanted to stay—I truly did—but I saw Amelia slipping out the door. I immediately ran after her and spotted her heading towards her vehicle. At an alarming speed, I was able to catch up to Amelia. I pinned her body against the car, slamming the door shut.

"Where do you think you are going?" I asked.

"You think you won?" she taunted as her eyes glinted with amusement. "Think again."

She stomped on my foot, and I yelped out in pain. This female was really pissing me off. I grabbed her broken arm and pulled hard. She cried out, as it was still healing. I pulled her towards me and threw a punch on her face. I broke her nose again.

Letting her go, I took a step back. "I am stronger than you, and I am luna to Titus. I am his rightful mate. I am his mate by Moon Goddess herself. The bond I have with him is stronger than yours."

"You wish," she spat at me.

"No, I don't. Moon Goddess herself blessed me with this bond." I taunted as I moved around her in circles. "One truer than their hearts, one where resistance will be futile, one that is stronger and will not depart. Together, they will become the ultimate mates—bonded by fate for eternity. A bond stronger than all, a bond that has always been tied as one."

"What the hell does that mean?" she asked.

My lips curled into a smile as I looked at her with clear intentions. "At first, I didn't understand it too, but I did just like she told me. I opened my mind and my heart. It means that my bond was purer and truer than yours. My bond has surpassed yours, and he is mine. He was always mine, to begin with. I am not afraid. I will win this fight, and I will enjoy killing you."

She snickered hysterically before shifting into her wolf form; it gave her more strength. She pushed herself off her paws and came at me. Caught by surprise, I fell to the ground. I quickly shifted into mine, and before she could snap at my neck, I beat her to it, clamping her down hard. I used one of my hind legs to kick her off. She flew back and fell onto the ground with a whimper. I shifted into my human form, standing tall and completely naked in front of her as my eyes locked onto my prey. I burst into a run, and as soon as Amelia saw me coming, she stood up. She pushed herself off her hind legs, and I kicked myself up into a jump. We met each other halfway through the air where I extended my claws and grabbed her by her throat. She mewled and clawed at my hands as we landed on the ground. I could feel her blood seeping down my hand.

I pulled her face close to mine. "I win."

In one swift movement, I pulled hard and ripped her head off. Blood spurted on my skin, producing a gurgling sound as she died in front of me. I dropped what I ripped from her and stared at her dead body.

It wasn't until I heard Titus call my name was when I zoned out from staring at Amelia. His hands were cupping my face as he shouted my name, shaking me slightly.

"That's it. Look at me," he said, soothing me. I blinked several times before nodding.

"I killed her," I whispered, almost not recognizing my voice.

"Yes, you did," he said as he nodded, pulling my face into his chest and wrapping his arms around me. I hugged him back limply. "You're okay. You're fine now."

Noor came up with a blanket, and Titus wrapped it around me. We got into the vehicle that Amelia used to bring us here and drove back to the pack house. When we arrived, Titus carried me upstairs and to the bathroom where he put me in the tub and began cleaning me up. He lathered up a sponge and began washing away the blood. I sat in the tub and allowed him to do it.

I trained relentlessly in Alpha Kyle's pack, but I had never been sent out to kill. Amelia was the first person I had killed. The look in her eyes when I took her life haunted me, but my wolf was actually purring in delight. I knew she liked the idea of eliminating what would threaten our bond with Titus.

"Talk to me, Patience." Titus pleaded after he finished bathing me and pulled me up to dry me.

"I killed someone today. Even if it was Amelia . . . I am not used to it," I responded. He nodded and wrapped the towel around me before placing a hand behind my head and bringing my forehead against his, our eyes meeting.

"You did what you had to do."

"Did I? I could've let her go," I reasoned.

"And she could've come back and killed you. Even if you were to let her go, I wouldn't have let her go. She would be dead regardless." Titus reasoned, and I nodded.

He moved to touch the scars on my face and neck, and his face darkened. I moved my forehead away from him and placed it on his chest to stop him from feeling angry. He hugged me tightly for a moment before he ushered me out of the shower to get dressed as he also took a shower. When he was done, he came out with a towel wrapped around his waist. He was in the middle of drying his hair when he saw me sitting on the bed. He walked over and sat next to me.

"I have something to say," I said.

166

"What is it?" he replied.

"Kailyn called and spoke to Kyle. He is letting her go." Titus looked slightly panicked, and I sought to remove what I knew he feared.

"I don't think he is coming for me, but I just wanted to let you know," I murmured, and he nodded before moving me to his lap. The closeness of him comforted me tremendously. "I also have something else to say."

He pulled back, and a frown came on his face. I shifted in his lap to get comfortable, but he tightened his grip on me. I turned to look at him, and he shook his head. The apparent hardness underneath me told me exactly why. I made an 'O' with my mouth before nodding.

"What is it that you needed to say?" he asked.

I told him about the Moon Goddess visiting me. He listened intently and was quiet after. I realized I must sound crazy telling him this, and I was just starting to think he would not believe me, but he quickly interrupted my thoughts.

"I had heard about these kinds of dreams when I was little. My father and the council members that were close to us used to tell us about them," he said before he grinned and looked at me. "So that means my bond tops Kyle's."

I rolled my eyes and moved to get off his lap. He rolled me underneath him on the bed. His towel completely loosened now as he did so. I placed my palms on his chest. He leaned down and pecked me on the lips before kissing my scars gently. The slow cool tingling sensation of his touch was easing the pain.

He did it until all the pain was gone and my eyes grew sleepy. I struggled to keep them open, and when I felt Titus moving away from me, my hands tightened around his shoulders.

"Don't leave me," I whispered.

"I never will," he replied softly. "I just need to get dressed, and then I'll come to bed."

I nodded and let him go. I allowed sleep to take over and when I felt the bed shift under me, I knew he came back to bed. My body crawled closer to him. He moved to kiss my forehead as I adjusted myself so that I was again half on top of him.

"I'm thinking about officially making you mine."

"Didn't you already do that?" I drowsily asked as I nuzzled my face into his chest, loving the feel of him against my cheek.

He chuckled. "I mean, I am thinking about doing a mating ceremony."

CHAPTER 31

A couple of days later, the news of what happened had traveled through the pack. Many were not surprised by the outcome. I still struggled at times with the fact that I did really end a life. I trained all my life to fight, but never had I killed.

It might seem like a brutal act, but in the werewolf world, we see things differently. Sometimes, things are a lot grayer than what we expect. We also can't ignore the fact that we are born with our other half as an animal. We are predators to the outside world. We are lethal and dangerous.

There were nights I would wake up frightened and sweaty. Titus was with me through it all. It was not so long ago that it seemed finding love was impossible, but now, not anymore.

I sat on a picnic blanket and watched Titus and his pack play a battle strategy game on the field. Kailyn had gone home with Micah. She seemed well and happy after the traumatic event. I think it takes losing someone to realize how much they really meant. She was troubled with her loyalty to Kyle and her fate to her destined mate.

I couldn't imagine how life would be if Kyle had decided he wanted me and left Kailyn. Would I have met Titus? Probably not. I didn't want to change a thing. I loved my life the way it is right now. I loved my mate who was on the field, fighting.

After the fight was over, Titus walked over and dropped to lay down on the blanket. His head lay comfortably on my lap as he looked up at me. I smoothed back his dark black hair and gazed into his cerulean eyes, which only confirmed my thoughts earlier.

"I can't imagine a life without you," I whispered.

His smile grew wide, and he moved to slip my hair behind my ear before cupping my cheeks. I closed my eyes as warmth and tingles spread through my body by his touch. The love in my heart grew even more.

"And the same goes for me," he replied before trailing his thumb on my bottom lip, leaving a wake of goosebumps on my skin. He always had this effect on me.

He must've smelled my arousal because he flipped onto his hands and knees and proceeded to push me back. The hunger in his eyes glinted wickedly. By now, everyone had dispersed from the field, leaving their alpha and luna alone.

He pushed me onto my back before covering my body with his. I wrinkled my nose.

"You are sweaty," I whined and tried to push him off me.

"Don't act like you don't like it. I know you do," he teased.

I bit my lips to stop the smile that was growing on my face. His face hovered over mine before his eyes stared down to my lips. My heart pounded against my ribcage. I wanted to jump out and throw myself into Titus's arms.

"You know, Patience, I did win that battle on the field a moment ago. I think I deserve a victory kiss." A slow, mischievous smile appeared on his face before he leaned down. I stopped the kiss from happening by blocking it with my hands. He pulled back with a frown.

"A kiss always leads to something, Titus." I giggled.

"And that is bad because?" He arched an eyebrow. His upper body was held up by his forearms so he could get a good look at me.

"Because we are out in the open!" I pushed him off me, but Titus wrapped his arms tightly around me and ended up rolling down the hill together.

I squealed and closed my eyes. When we were halfway down the hill, he let out a painful groan. My eyes opened to see that his back had hit a large and pointed rock.

"Patience, I am in pain. I need a kiss to take away the ache." He feigned weakness.

I laughed before giving him what he wanted. My upper body was on top of his, and I leaned down to kiss him on the lips. He was beginning to be very spoiled, but I had to admit I did enjoy loving this male of mine.

A throat clearing got our attention. I pushed away from Titus only to have his arms tightened around me. We turned to look and saw Christian smiling down at us. His eyes sparkled with amusement.

"At this rate, you two will get pregnant before Emily and me," Christian commented.

"Or we can get pregnant at the same time!" Emily chirped from behind Christian. She peeked behind his back to look at Titus and me.

"Titus, let me go." A heated blush spanned all over my cheeks. It was embarrassing to be caught by pack members in such a compromising situation and to also have them think about getting pregnant already.

"I think that isn't a bad idea, Christian. I think I better get to work right now. This pack needs another little alpha running around." Titus grinned and wiggled his eyebrows at me.

I swatted his chest playfully. "Can you just stop teasing?"

He laughed heartily. "I'll let you go if you kiss me."

I rolled my eyes as Christian and Emily laughed. Titus was really spoiled. Eventually, he did end up letting me go. Once Titus did, Emily took hold of my hand.

"Patience, let's go shopping. We have a lot of things to prepare for the mating ceremony. You know, we need to look at the food that we will have at the ceremony, and we also need to get

171

the decorations. It will be an amazing night," Emily said eagerly. "Plus, we can't forget the most important person—you. We need to find you a dress perfect for your mating ceremony. Soon, you will officially be Alpha Titus's mate."

"She's already officially mine," Titus remarked from the ground.

Christian chortled, and I scoffed. "Not until you catch me, I am not."

His eyes darkened with anticipation and pleasure. "Patience, you know that I will catch you, and when I do, you will be mine. It will be easy. I have done it at the hunting game, and I will do it again."

The memories of the hunting game brought a smile to my face. I remembered the first time I met him. He killed another male to get to me. Possessive and dominating.

"Confident, eh?" I asked. "I am counting on you catching me, Titus."

He pushed himself off the grass in an attempt to grab hold of my wrist, but I jumped out of his way. Laughing, I took hold of Emily's hand and ran up the hill towards the pack house. I needed to plan.

CHAPTER 32

Tonight, the moon was shining down brightly in acceptance to the individuals who were awake below, celebrating. It was as if the Moon Goddess herself was blessing the ceremony. Faint small light bulbs hung on strings from the trees around the open ground of Titus's pack territory. The pack members stood, watching with excited smiles on their faces. It was a moment they were honored to witness, the only mating ceremony for their alpha and the formal introduction of their luna. Standing in a long dark red dress that touched the ground and a low v-neck that covered enough to keep me decent but left enough to entice Titus, I looked ahead at who was in front of me.

He was shirtless with a pair of black trousers. The pack tattoo and alpha symbol on his arm was proudly displayed for everyone to see. His black hair slicked back neatly as he watched me with his piercing cerulean eyes. That male in front of me was really all mine. Without speaking out loud, his eyes began beckoning me forward, and as if my body knew what he wanted, I followed. When I was close enough to him, he moved to take hold of my hand, leading me up to stand before him on equal ground.

His other hand came up to place two fingers under my chin, and then he lifted my gaze to his. His eyes held so much warmth and love. It made me feel fuzzy and happy. Out of everything in my life, he was the only choice I had full confidence in.

"You're beautiful," he whispered huskily, and I felt heat crawling on my cheeks at his compliment. A grin appeared on his face as he wrapped one arm around my shoulders, turning us to the crowd.

"Tonight, we celebrate not just my mating but also having our luna and the union of our pack. We are now stronger than ever," he began, and everyone howled and hooted.

He turned to me. His arm that was around my shoulder now slipped down to my waist, pulling me up against him possessively. The other hand moved my hair back, exposing my neck and his mark. His eyes flitted back up to me, and I could see the pride that reflected in those stunning irises.

"You are my second chance and my moon, Patience," he spoke. "I promise to love and care for you. You are my second half, my lover, and my forever mate. I will love you, hold you, and honor you for the rest of our lives."

My breath caught in my throat at his sweet words. His lips came down on mine as he pulled my bottom lip in between his. "I love you and only you, Patience, with all my heart."

His lips moved down my jawline to my neck where I felt his canine elongating and piercing my skin—marking me again, but the proper way this time. Our souls and werewolf spirits danced inside of us as our bond strengthened even more. I closed my eyes against the tingling sensation rippling through my veins. It was like he was invading my body and knowing everything about it.

When he pulled back, his eyes were pitch black with desire. Nervously, I took in my bottom lip between my teeth before I summoned enough courage to move and cup his cheeks. I pulled him down to kiss him, letting him know that he was the one for me and how much I loved him. The feel of his canine was still evident, but it only turned me on more. When I finally pulled back, it was my turn to speak.

"I love you too, Titus," I said as I caressed his cheek. His eyes were never leaving mine. "You are my second chance at love, my second chance at life. You are my one and only alpha. I will love you forever. I promise to respect, care, and be attentive towards you. Titus, this is my sacred vow to you. You are mine."

I brought him down for another hard kiss before moving to the side of his neck where my mark was. With my canine lengthening, I moved in and pierced my mark again on his neck. The sweet metallic rush of blood flooded my mouth, and it only encouraged me to dig my canines deeper. A soft groan escaped his lips as his arms tightened around me. He liked what I was doing. I could feel the hardness of his erection pressed against my belly. When I finished, I lapped at his mark to clean it up before pulling back, licking my lips. His eyes were still the color of the dark night as he looked at me.

Everyone cheered and began howling. Smiling, I pushed away from Titus's grasp. His eyes were still on me as I moved away from him. The females giggled as they did the same. When I was with the other females, I turned and we broke into a run, lifting our dresses as we shifted in the air. I heard Titus's throaty, dominating growl from behind along with other males as they began their chase. It was a growl that promised a chase that he would win—a chase that he was thrilled to follow.

"Run, Patience, because when I catch you, you will be mine," he shouted, and I felt a tug in my heart and warmth pooled between my legs. I had no doubt that Titus would catch me. I was counting that he would, but I'd make damn sure it wouldn't be easy for him.

I dashed through the dark woods, my eyes quickly adjusting to the change in environment. I was able to see shadows, shapes, and movements even without light. It was like seeing through a night vision scope. I could only see enough for me to be able to hunt and see my way around at night.

Titus would shift into his wolf as soon as he hit the edge of the woods. His senses would be heightened, and he would for sure follow his female's scent. I ducked under a fallen log and burrowed my way through some thick bushes

I could hear the paws of the other female wolves next to me who were running away from their mates. My plan was to mask my scent as much as possible. I rubbed my scent on a few trees and bushes to deter Titus from me. Once I was able to send him in a direction that would be safe for me, I did a 180 and headed for the stream on their territory.

This water would lessen my scent, and it would be harder for him to find me. I trotted along the stream searching for a place to hide. It felt like the first time at the Hunting Game, only this time, I was fully aware of who was chasing me.

My paws dug into the earthy mud with each step I took. I reached a small cave near the stream. Water was trickling down the cave. This could be a good spot to hide. I walked inside and shifted into my human form, fully aware that I was naked.

The cave was damp with an earthy muddy smell. It knew that it would be a lot harder for Titus to find me here. Approaching the end of the cave where there was no exit, I found a fleece blanket nicely folded in a corner. People must have hidden here before. Picking it up, I wrapped around my shoulders, shielding my nakedness from the cold.

"Cold?" A thrilling shiver ran down my spine. Excitement bubbled up in my stomach and my heart fluttered like I was falling in love all over again.

He was here.

I turned to face him, giving him a rewarding smile. "Found me."

He stood before me fully naked. He was unashamed. He stood proudly in front of me in the most provocative and dominating stance. He returned my smile with a victorious and confident smirk before slowly walking towards me.

I took a step back.

He arched an eyebrow. "Still running?"

"Still chasing?" I shot back, feeling a lot more playful. I knew I was teasing him, and he enjoyed it.

"Always," he whispered before moving closer to me, capturing me in his arms tightly. My shivering body was now firmly pressed onto his hard one.

"You were sneaky, Patience," he whispered huskily as his lips grazed my cheeks. It was a soft caress.

"Yet you still found me." I managed to breathe in a bare whisper. It was always hard to think around him.

"I will always find you, love." His lips found their way back to mine.

He brushed his lips over mine before deepening the kiss; the unquenchable flame inside

of me burst to life. I let go of the blanket to wrap my arms around him, my hands moving to tangle with his hair. He groaned with pleasure and deepened the kiss even more. I could feel his arousal pressing against me.

It didn't take long for Titus to spread out the blanket and place me carefully in the middle of it. Tonight, he was going to make me his again officially. Tonight, in the eyes of the moon and our goddess, our mating was going to be complete.

Titus moved his body to cover mine. Every inch of his skin touched my already burning body. I moaned and wrapped my legs around his waist. He leaned down to give me a passionate and deep kiss before moving his lips lower. He nipped at his mark on my neck before I felt the grazing of his canines.

I thought he was going to mark me again right then, but instead, he moved lower. His kisses were feathering my skin to the valley of my breasts. I arched my back, wanting more. He took mercy on me and cupped one breast with his hands, squeezing it before pinching the tip.

His lips latched onto my other breast where he flicked and teased the bead until I was writhing underneath him, begging for some form of release between my legs.

"I want to take my time with you tonight. I want to taste every single part of your body. I want to know what makes you cry out my name, and I want to know what will drive you to the edge of pleasurable insanity." His voice was husky with want.

As Titus promised, he made damn sure that his promise that night was followed

through. He made love to me in a way that had me crying out in pleasure and begging him for release. He learned everything about me, and by the time the sun peeked over the horizon, I was exhausted, and my body was humming with satisfaction.

I spent years living a life filled with pain and rejection until I met Titus. He changed my life forever, and I thank the Moon Goddess every day for the gift she has given me. He was the light and my chance at happiness. He gave me hope and dreams, and I knew I couldn't love anybody more. He was my heart, my love, and my mate.

EPILOGUE

A year later

I can't believe it has been a year since everything happened—a year since I was officially mated to the French alpha who is absolutely possessive and protective of me.

Time has flown by; Kailyn and Micah have also settled into their relationship. The mating ceremony for them was held six months after ours. By then, Kailyn was already pregnant with male twins.

Now, the babies are a few months old and already loved by the pack. Micah loves and adores Kailyn. My sister often calls me and tells me that she is happy she made this choice. There are days she thinks about Kyle, but he seems to be only a distant memory, a person from her past.

She told me she doesn't hate him. She was angry that he kept all this to himself and didn't tell her. She was angry that she allowed him to mark her when he was supposed to be mine. Kailyn now knows that I have already forgiven her. I am happy about where I am.

I am happy with the man I love.

Titus is everything to me. He takes extremely good care of me. Our love hasn't dimmed a bit but only continues to bloom. I have learned more French since I have convinced Titus to hire me a French teacher.

Christian and Emily are also very happy. It was great news to everyone when they heard that Emily and I are going to give birth to babies around the same time.

Yes, I am pregnant with Titus's baby. Standing in his office, I rest my hand on my protruding belly. He is working through some paperwork while I stay by his side.

I can't do anything else now that I have a baby growing inside of me. I feel the need to be close to Titus because he provides me comfort. As every other pregnant woman will say, as the time approaches, we often find ourselves

feeling anxious and fearful of what will happen. Going into labor scares me. I don't know what to expect, and having Titus near me will reassure me everything will be fine.

I sigh and think about Kyle. I truly hope that he finds happiness someday. I haven't spoken to him for a long time. I want him to move on, and I want to move on. In order for me to move on though, I need to not talk to him. I need time to forgive him.

Then my thoughts travel to Noor. Oh goddess, the thought of Titus's gamma being gone for so long hurts my heart. I wonder what is going on with him. He has become a very fast friend to me, and I have to admit I worry for his safety and his whereabouts.

Turning to face my mate who is working hard on finishing some pack paperwork to spend the day with me, I feel the need to express to him the urgency of finding Noor.

"He hasn't come home, Titus. You need to go find him," I muttered as I place the phone back on the receiver. Noor has been gone, and we haven't received word from him. I am beginning to worry.

"Who?" He looks confused.

"Gamma Noor," I respond impatiently.

"He is fine. If something is wrong, he will call me." Titus sets his papers down as he moves around his desk to wrap his arms around my waist. His hands slowly caress my protruding stomach.

"You shouldn't worry so much. You are pregnant with our little pup," he murmurs as he nips at my earlobe.

"All I am saying is if you don't go out there and find him or get him to call you, I am going out there myself." I threaten. He sighs and drops his forehead on my shoulder.

"Patience, please. He is fine," Titus says in an exasperated tone.

I turn around to look at him. My stomach pushes us apart as I do so. He frowns but keeps his arms around me.

"How do you know?" I ask.

"I just do," Titus mumbles, but I can see the uncertainty in his eyes.

"Don't lie to me, Titus," I reply.

He sighs. "Fine. I will send a couple of warriors out to search for him. Now will you please stop being a worrywart?"

Satisfied that I have won this conversation, I turn back around and allow him to pull me back into his embrace, his hands settling on top of my belly.

"You always win these fights." He pouts.

"Because you love me," I reply.

I can feel him smiling as he speaks, "I do. I love you with everything that I have."

"Promise me you will try to see where Noor is."

"I promise, my little Luna," he replies. "Now, let's go get you something to eat? I am sure our little pup is hungry. She's going to grow just as strong as her mother."

"Or her dad," I respond but allow him to pull me out of the office and downstairs.

During my time with Kyle, I never thought I would get this chance to be happy again, and now my life is completely perfect. I am married to a French alpha who is temperamental and possessive but loving. He is everything to me, and I can't imagine life without him.

I stop and pull his arm. He turns to look at me confused. I move and kiss him on the lips.

"I love you, Titus."

He smiles. "I love you too, Patience."

His lips come back down and kiss me again. It's passionate and sensual. His tongue slips out to dance with mine. My hands tighten around his neck. The alpha has other plans before food; of that I am sure by the way his arms wrap around me and the deep rumbling coming from his chest. My male wants something else before food. Well, I guess eating can wait.

Do you like werewolf stories?
Here are samples of other stories
you might enjoy!

ALPHA'S DIRTY LITTLE SECRET

SYMONE R.

CHAPTER 1

AMIRA

Gazing at the several unknown faces, I began to feel as if I was living in the shadows once again. I was left bearing a secret that made me feel like I was living in a lie.

Innocent humans watched as our college professor continued to lecture about Accounting and Finance. I looked to my left; beside me was a girl. Her blonde hair was draped over her brown eyes as she continued to scribble insignificant pictures on her notebook. What amazed me the most was how unaware she was of the nonhuman creature seated only inches away from her.

She sighed. My useful heightened senses allowed me to listen to her heartbeat and breathing that would accelerate every time the professor searched for a student to answer a simple question. Her heart rate would regulate once the professor called someone else. She slouched in her chair, her eyes occasionally wandering off from her work to a boy sitting in the far corner of the room.

"Amira? Are you paying attention?" I looked to my right, finding the eyes of my friend, Eric.

Eric and I have been friends since we were thirteen. Six years later, we were still going strong. We had a lot of classes together over the years, so our friendship continued to grow. However, despite us being friends, I could never find it in myself to tell him who I really was. Or should I say, *what* I was.

"Yeah...no," I admitted before we both shared a low snicker.

"Eric, you know I got all of this stuff already," I reassured him, slouching down in my chair.

I was known to be very intelligent in school. Unlike most, it was very easy for me to remember and comprehend any given task. This skill has been very helpful to me.

"Well, then, if it's so damn easy for you, you can teach it all to me because I'm lost as hell." Eric sighed. His eyes narrowed in on the textbook in front of him as I chuckled at him.

"Okay, ladies and gentlemen, class dismissed," the teacher announced as she wrapped up her lecture. I stood from my desk. Students began gathering their things before everyone scrambled out of the door.

"So, lunch on me today?" Eric offered.

"No, sorry. I have to help my mom prepare for this dinner we are having tomorrow. Just a few out-of-town guests." I sighed heavily.

"Okay, cool. Well, I'll text you tonight?"

"Sure."

*   *   *

The appetizing smell of food danced its way around me, clouding my nasal passages with the mouth-watering aroma of my mother's home-cooked meal.

I walked into the kitchen to see my mother running back and forth. She was cutting vegetables, stirring food in the pots, and measuring the temperature of whatever she was roasting in the oven.

"Mom, is it this serious?" She was acting as if the president was stopping by for dinner.

"Yes, sweetie. This is when you'll see your new alpha for the first time." My mother was more cheerful than the rest of us were.

It was amusing how my mother cared about the alpha's arrival more than the actual werewolves that lived here. I expected her to feel uncaring about his presence as if he was just another regular visitor, her being a human and all.

I guess being married to and being the mother of a werewolf really had her interested in the supernatural world. Unlike her, I couldn't care less about the werewolf society. I found human life to be much better. Accepting. I enjoyed not living under the command and authority of some male who was determined to show his dominance over everyone because of a title.

That was why I loved living in the city. Majority of our pack, including the alpha and beta, lived far out in the country somewhere.

Honestly, that's how I liked it. I loved being away from the group who allowed their title to get to their overgrown skull.

I preferred the distance. However, my father seemed to not feel the same way I do. Recently, he had invited the previous alpha and luna, and their son—the new alpha—over for dinner. Only my father could ruin such a beautiful thing.

"But Mom, they aren't coming until tomorrow," I reminded her again.

"I know, I know, but I prefer to get things done now."

I sighed. Looking over everything, I could see how she had handled things.

"You seem to have everything done." The chicken was roasting in the oven; the vegetables were boiling in the pots; and she seemed to be starting on dessert. "Call me if you need anything then."

I snatched up my bag from the kitchen counter. Reaching into the cupboard, I pulled a granola bar from the box before I left the kitchen.

I silently cursed my mother and father again. I don't even know why I have to be here. If I could, I would disappear before the guests even made it to town. Sadly, my father requested that I should be present for the attendees.

Why did I seem so against the presence of the new alpha? I would say our past was just a tiny piece of the reason that I wanted to disappear. Even though my mother said it's the first time meeting the new alpha, it's actually not. We had already met before he had taken over the title, alpha.

When I was about eight years old, my father and I would visit the main pack house for some business. Since my father was one of the strongest warriors of our pack, the previous alpha would need him by his side during decision-making.

That's when I had first met eleven-year-old Xavier, the soon-to-be alpha.

My father said—to keep us busy and out of their hair while he helped the alpha—Xavier and I should go play, and we did. Honestly, I thought Xavier was cute. I was actually very fond of him. Stupidly, I asked him if he felt the same way. Let's just say it was not the answer I hoped for.

To impress his friends, who were the children of other higher ranked members, he knocked me off the swing. I remembered crying on the ground as he and the other kids laughed before they left me soaking in my own tears.

That fucking bitch.

Yes, I knew that it happened many years ago, but for some reason, I just couldn't forget and forgive. I guess I just didn't take rejection or embarrassment too well. I still don't.

Luckily, after that, I never saw him again, and I was perfectly fine with it.

I quickly shook the thoughts off before I disappeared into the bathroom.

I stood in front of the mirror in my room after I finished taking a shower. I ran my hands down my hips as I stared at my reflection. I adored my frame. I didn't consider myself fit or slim like the other female werewolves I had encountered. Other she-wolves had a fit and athletic physique, the type of body that would look exceptional in anything. I, on the other hand, did not have that. I was a curvaceous woman—full breasts, thick hips and thighs without such a slim waist. I would always assure myself that I would soon diet. At least, after I finish off the pizza I was enjoying.

I began to smile. My full pink lips looked well with my silky smooth skin and brown eyes.

I pulled out my blow dryer and started drying my shoulder-length black hair. When my hair was already dry, I pinned it up and leaped into my bed. Turning my television on, I searched through various channels until I finally landed on a show I could finish my night with.

*   *   *

Wrapped up in my comforter, I felt at ease. No classes. No early morning wake-up calls. Just the perfect time to oversleep.

"Amira, wake up. Let's go the mall." I heard my mother's all too familiar voice as she pushed through my bedroom door.

"No, thank you," I rolled away from her. "It's too early."

"Too early? It's 12:30 in the afternoon. Now, get your butt up."

I turned to my mother and an annoyed snarl escaped me. She narrowed her eyes and shot me a warning glare before walking away. It was a warning, convincing me that her wrath was more powerful than my teeth.

"Make it an hour, or I'm coming back."

"Fine." I sighed.

I stayed in bed for another fifteen minutes; I just did not want to get up. Mustering up some energy, I swung my legs and sat up from the bed. Tired and drained, I dragged myself to my bathroom.

After finishing my routine, I picked up my bag and made my way downstairs.

"Hey, Dad," I greeted my father as I walked into the kitchen. He glanced up from his paper to meet my gaze.

"Hey, where are you two headed?"

"She's dragging me to the mall." I slipped into a chair beside him. I reached for his paper and pulled the comic section from the crumbled pile.

"Oh, good luck." I could sense the humor in his comment.

My father knew how things went when it involved accompanying my mother to the mall. He had found a way to get out of it. During their mall trips, he would make her shopping experience hell. He complained, dragged his feet, and gave opinions my mother found useless. Occasionally, he would become 'ill' during their mall runs.

I could only admire his tactics for escaping.

"Okay, sweetie, I'm ready."

"Okay." I sighed and stood up from my chair.

I followed my mother out to the car and got in. I slumped down in my seat as I listened to the vehicle's engine roar to life from under the hood. I slipped my earbuds on and drifted into my own thoughts the entire ride.

*   *   *

We roamed the mall for hours, not looking for a specific item. My mother just wanted to buy random things. With the help of my complaints, my mother wrapped up her shopping journey, and we finally left the mall.

"Sweetie, can you tell your father to come help with the bags?" I scowled at her. *What am I? A personal beeper?*

Reaching into our mind link, I urged for his assistance. A few seconds later, my father emerged from the front entrance. He grabbed my mother's bag, refusing to have her carry her own.

He should have joined us in our mall run then. With his petty whining, I would have been home already.

By the time we arrived home, I made my way to the kitchen and walked over to the refrigerator, pulling a bottle of water from the shelf. As I turned to leave, I witnessed my parents sharing an intimate kiss in the living room. "We all have rooms for that, people."

"Sorry, honey." My mother's cheeks flushed red as she pulled away from my father.

"You will understand once you find your mate," my father explained.

A mate. To us werewolves, our mate would be someone the moon goddess has blessed us with. A mate would be someone we plan to spend the rest of eternity with.

Love. A destined bond that was almost unavoidable and hard to break. My mother and father were mates. He shared his secret with her, and she accepted his life and him as well.

However, some weren't that blessed. Some were cursed. Some were given a mate who could be careless, cold-blooded, and downright disgraceful.

There could be some who don't want a mate. Some who would rather remain unrestricted than fall into the spell of the mate bond.

Rejection. Some would rather reject their mate; it's their way of freeing themselves from the world they consider a prison. However, it's not always accepted by the other. The rejected mate may not fully accept it, leaving them with a broken heart and the feeling of desertion. Some would begin to feel as though it's their own actions that caused the rejection, and feel self-loathe and hatred for their wolves. Finally, another dangerous aspect was pain, hatred, and even suicidal ideation.

Honestly, I didn't care about finding my mate. I didn't want to find some wolf who probably believed that I my only purpose was to bear his children and sleep with him. A man who would probably only use me as his chew toy. I couldn't allow someone to have so much control over me, so much power. And then give me so much heartache.

"No, thank you on the mate thing, Dad." A waved my hands frantically. I didn't want that curse.

"Honey, go, get dressed. Our guests should be arriving in about an hour." My mom pressed.

Shifting my eyes toward my father, I shot him a venomous glare once again.

"Oh, honey, you will love them. They are nice people, so relax."

Disagreeing with him, I picked up the small bags I had gotten from the mall and ran up to my room to prepare for an unwanted arrival.

If you enjoyed this sample, look for
Alpha's Dirty Little Secret
on Amazon.

MY SECOND CHANCE MATE

ANNA GONZALES

CHAPTER ONE
Rejected but Moving On

HARMONY

Waking up in the morning has never been easy for me and now it feels as if there's no point in doing it at all. I didn't always feel this way. I used to love life. I enjoyed hanging out with friends and even going to school. That changed the day I met my mate. What is a mate? It's supposed to be the best part of being a werewolf, which is what I am. We are born in human form and can transform into a wolf at the age of twelve. From that point on, it's a waiting game until we find our mate. A mate is a special someone who completes you; the one you was made for and vice versa. I should be happy to have found mine. Unfortunately, my story is unique and I don't mean that in a good way.

*   *   *

One Year Ago . . .

I met him at the age of sixteen. He was everything I could've hoped for. Seventeen years old, 6'1', gorgeous gray eyes, dark black hair, nicely tanned skin, washboard abs, and strong long legs. Perfect, right? I thought so too. We found each other outside the airport baggage claim area. Our eyes met and it was electrifying. We moved towards one another as if pulled by some force until we were only a foot away.

"Mate," we both whispered. He reached out to touch my cheek and I leant into his palm. It felt right; like home. I was so happy that I closed my eyes to savor the moment when he suddenly tensed and dropped his hand. I opened my eyes to ask what was wrong just as he took a big step back. I stared at him in confusion and was about to ask what made him move away when the sound of a familiar voice made the words freeze on my lips.

"Babe, I see you've met my sister. Isn't she adorable?" My older sister, Megan, gushed as she gave me her usual too-tight, can't breathe type of hug.

"Did you say babe?" I asked.

"Yes, silly! Aiden, you didn't introduce yourself?" She laughed while playfully swatting his chest. "Harmony, meet the best thing to come out of this whole mandatory wolf camp that mom and dad sent me to. My boyfriend, Aiden James," she announced happily while grabbing his arm.

My wolf growled at the sight of her touching my mate, but I couldn't say anything right now. I love my sister. She's my best friend and she looked so happy. I couldn't do anything to ruin that. Don't get me wrong;I had some serious questions to ask but I would get my answers when the time was right. Even if I had to tie Aiden to a chair to do it. There was a satisfactory rumble from my wolf just by picturing it. I couldn't believe that, out of all people my sister could have met at this camp, she had to meet and fall in love with the one wolf meant for me.

The camp they attended was a first of it's kind. It was created for two types of wolves. The first was for someone like Aiden, a future alpha. These types of wolves would one day be the leaders of their pack and had to be taught to control their added power and authority so that it wouldn't be misused. The second was for wolves born from two werewolf parents who both carry the recessive gene. It causes their child to be born completely human, and my sister was one of those children. The whole thing was complicated enough as it is, and finding out I was the mate of a future alpha my sister was currently dating only added to the complication.

Aiden and I quickly exchanged hellos as if the spine tingling encounter between us never happened. We grabbed their bags and headed to the car. The ride was uncomfortable mainly because the love birds decided to share the back seat and cuddle. I exchanged looks with Aiden a couple times in the mirror, and though he would smile at my sister, the looks he gave me seemed sad and resigned. His mood confused me but I expected to get an explanation soon.

We made it to our pack house where they were having a big barbeque to welcome my sister and Aiden back. Aiden is the only nephew of our alpha, and because our alpha's mate is human, she could not conceive a child. Our law states that the next male in line would be the alpha's younger brother, Aiden's dad. However, he was killed by rogues when Aiden was thirteen so by law, Aiden is the next heir. It is strange that we never had the opportunity to meet before but that's due to the fact that Aiden's mother took him back to her pack shortly after his father's death. She was unable to deal with the memories of her lost mate that surrounded her wherever she went. Her story was sad and was still used today to teach young pups the ups and downs of mating.

After about an hour into the barbeque, my sister made a run to the store with our mom, and it finally gave me a chance to get Aiden alone. I dragged him to a clearing, a little far down from our pack house, and laid above him.

"So, what are we going to do? I love my sister to death but we're mates. We can't deny that. I don't want to hurt her but the pull I feel for you is so strong I can't ignore it," I started rambling.

"I can," he said.

I continued, not quite hearing him. "I mean, I know this is going to be difficult and create a lot of drama but I'm so happy I've found you a—"

He cut me off and repeated those two words, loud enough so I could hear them. "I can."

"You can? Can what?" I asked, confused.

"I can ignore it. This pull between us," he stated. He proceeded to rip my heart out of my chest with the rest of his words. "I never had a choice in many things in my life. I didn't choose to lose my dad, or have to leave my pack, or be put into the role of alpha but I chose your sister. I fell in love with her all on my own with no influence from anyone. I refuse to change how I feel just because my wolf wants me to. I want to be with the one I love because I say so and not because a bond is forcing me to."

I stared at him. I was shocked and hurt. "Are you saying what I'm thinking? Are you rejecting our bond?"

He sighed. "Look, I don't want to hurt you, Harmony. I spent time with your sister, and I got to know her and fell in love all on my own. If I'm with you, it's not by choice anymore but by fate. I refuse to let fate control anything else in my life. I'm sorry but that's just how it has to be."

To say I was hurt was an understatement. What came next was just anger. "You refuse? What about me? Do you know how long I've dreamed of meeting my mate and finally feeling the love only he can give me? Only you can give me? And now you tell me I can never feel that because fate has dealt you a cruel hand and you're rebelling? And so I'm the one who has to pay for your misfortune? I have never done anything in my sixteen years of life to deserve that, but does it matter to you? Obviously not!" I cried out.

"Look, Harmony. I—"

"No, you look. I'm sorry you had to go through all that but that's what I can be here for. I can help heal the pain you've been through and support you through the role that was forced onto you. No one will be able to understand you like I, your mate, can. Let me do this for you. For us," I pleaded.

"I just can't, Harmony. I've already chosen the future I want, and that future is with your sister," he replied firmly.

"What about our bond? It's going to be hard to fight it. My wolf is trying to get through, and I'm sure so is yours. How are you going to deny him?" I questioned.

Nothing. And I meant nothing could have saved me from the pain his answer caused. "Well, I'll fight him off until I completely mate with Megan. Once I mark her, he will be easier to control, and as more time passes, our bond will eventually weaken."

"True, but you forgot one important detail. Or maybe it's not so important to you since you won't be affected but what happens to the rejected mate, Aiden? What will happen to me? Let me remind you, being that I don't have a choice in the rejection," I lashed out in anger, "my wolf will weaken. When you mark Megan, I will feel as if my chest has been ripped open. You will have your love for Megan to help get you through the weakened bond, but I won't be able to find another wolf mate since we are only given one in our lifetime. Even though the bond will deteriorate, I will still hurt every day. I will have to see you together and be reminded of my rejection time and time again. Is that really what you want for me? I know you feel something for me. I saw it at the airport. Are you absolutely sure this is what you want to do?"

"It's what I want," he whispered. "I've thought about this my whole life."

I tried one last plea."What about kids, Aiden? Megan is human. You won't be able to have a pup with her. How will you carry on your alpha line?"

"I'll deal with that when the problem arises."

"So you'll give up your mate and any future blood children just to spite fate?" I asked, hurt and shocked.

He nodded. "Yes. I'm really sorry. I just can't be with you." There was a hint of sadness in his voice.

"It's not that you can't. You just chose not to," I whispered in defeat. "So you're finally getting to choose for yourself, and that choice forces me into a life of pain and misery," I said as I looked him in the eyes. I thought I saw some indecision and pain, but it was quickly replaced by resignation and determination. I looked away as the tears started to fall. "Fine." I turned back to face him. "I will accept your rejection of the bond but only because like a mate should; I only want your happiness. You see, that's what mates are supposed to do: Protect each other, care for one another, and put each other first. I will endure the pain of the future for you, and I hope that it haunts you every night while you live your happily ever after with my sister." And with that said, I shifted into my light brown wolf and ran further into the darkness of the woods.

*   *   *

Shaking my head of the unwanted memories, I think about my life since then. I haven't done anything drastic to my appearance. I still wear my brown hair long and straight, no contacts cover my light green eyes, my full lips are still only covered in clear lip gloss, and I haven't changed from skinnys and tanks to ripped jeans and grungy t-shirts. No, the only change is my attitude.

The sweet carefree nature is gone. I now know how real life can be and it isn't a fairytale. My enthusiasm for life is gone. When you look into my eyes, you'll see emptiness that hides the constant pain.

I no longer live with my pack. Six months after my rejection, Aiden marked my sister and the pain was unbearable. I couldn't be around him and see him happy anymore. Yes, there were times when I was near him and could feel his wolf fighting for control but Aiden always pushed him back. I begged my parents to let me leave the pack and join my maternal aunt's pack— Her mate's pack in Hawaii, to be specific. My parents didn't understand why at first because I never told anyone about my rejection. I made up the excuse of it being hard to be around Aiden and Megan knowing I haven't found my mate yet. At least it was half true.

That's where I am now. A new pack, a new school, and hopefully, a new life. I should have an optimistic attitude, but I no longer have the illusion of happily ever after. Hope is something I seriously lack in the present. There is one good thing to come from all this.

"Harmony, get your lazy ass up so we can get to school. I don't want to miss all the fresh meat awaiting me. My game is on fire today. Just don't stare too hard at me 'cause you might be blinded by all this hotness."

There it is. My cousin Jared. He's the only one who knows about my rejection because, unlike my aunt and uncle, I can't hide the pain from him. He knows me too well, and it took all of my wolf strength to stop him from jumping on a plane to beat the crap out of Aiden. It's good though because he constantly takes my mind off of things with his crazy man whorish ways and wise remarks. His friends are awesome too. And are total eye candies. A few tried hitting on me when I was first introduced to the pack, but Jared gave all them death glares. He warned his player friends that I was completely hands off unless any of them were planning on putting a ring on my finger. I laughed at all the deathly ill expressions in the room after that announcement. Commitment is equal to a bad case of crabs in their minds. I can't wait 'til they meet their mates. It'll be fun watching them get tamed.

I get dressed in some black skinnys and an off-shoulder white top with a black tank underneath. I put my hair in a loose bun, gloss my lips, and slip into a pair of black gladiator sandals. As I'm tucking a fly away hair behind my ear, the opening of the front door announces Jace, Nate, and Brad's arrival. I make my way to their voices and find them in the kitchen as usual.

"Bro, I'm telling you. This year we're gonna score so much pu—"

"Lady in the room!" I shout, interrupting what I'm sure was gonna be one of Nate's more colorful terms for *vajayjay*.

"Right. Sorry, Harm. As I was saying, we're gonna score so much chicks because we're now seniors," Nate corrects himself excitedly.

"Well, I know I will, but I'm not too sure about you ugly mutts. Just don't stand too close to me and you'll have a chance since my sex appeal is just too massive," Jared boasts, a l in his usual arrogant self.

"Really, Jared? I know what's massive about you, and it's not your sex appeal or your weiner. Don't try to deny it. Our moms showered us together when we were little, and if I remember correctly, which I do, it was very, very, very tiny," I say, making sure I emphasized the size with my thumb and pointer fingers.

"Hey, that's because I haven't changed yet. Trust me. Massive isn't even a big enough word to describe it now," he argues, a tiny bit offended.

I cringe. "First of all, gross. And second, your ego is the only thing that's massive. I'm worried if you don't bring it down you might not be able to fit your fat head out the door."

"She's right. Besides, we all know my sexiness outshines all of you," Brad informs them.

"No way. I score the most ass . . . I mean chicks every year," Jace argues.

"That's only cause you don't have standards and will screw anything with two sets of lips," says Nate with a raised brow.

This sets off a whole new conversation about what's doable and what's not, followed by pushing and headlocks. These boys are too much and, even though I'm not excited about the day ahead, it promises to be entertaining.

If you enjoyed this sample, look for
My Second Chance Mate
on Amazon.

HIS MOON

MAGGIE MCNEILL

CHAPTER 1
Wood Smoke and Fir Trees

Kaia had stopped being afraid of the dark a long time ago. One day, she woke up thirsty in the middle of the night and quietly walked through the dark, creaky house, forgetting to flip on all of the lights she usually did. She didn't need them.

She learned that there were much better things to fear than the dark.

Looking back, she couldn't remember exactly when it was that she stopped sleeping with the shades open so that the moonlight could glide into her room, illuminating her pillow and keeping her safe. It happened sometime after Kaia's mom had died.

Like Kaia said, there were better things to fear than the dark—like death or loneliness.

☾

Kaia shivered even though she had a cup of hot chocolate snug between her hands. She took a sip to shake off the rest of the strange feeling that washed over her.

She'd been feeling off all day, thinking about grim things. But that was to be expected. It was the anniversary of her mom's murder. She was sitting alone in her usual coffee shop, listening to music and pretending the world didn't exist for a moment. She needed a break from Cole and her dad. Hot chocolate and music was the solution.

She had that dream again, the same one that she always had around this time of the year. The world grew cold, and so did Kaia's heart. She was tired of it. The dream just made things hurt more. It wasn't like the usual ones she had. It felt like a series of emotions following each other: a love of the sort she'd never known, a sharp blade of anger, and an empty echo of pain. The darkness she experienced every time she had that dream was painful to look at, somehow blinding despite being devoid of any light.

Kaia's phone lit up, vibrating on her rickety little table. She squinted at the screen and saw a message from 'Papa.'

Get home, or I'm coming to get you.

Kaia sighed. He would, too. He knew where she was—always did. So much for a break. She shook her head, staring at her pale hands. She wished to whoever was listening that she'd one day be able to pry the world open with those hands and dig out the treasures it had to offer. She wanted to *live*.

But such a feat seemed hard when she had a dad who barely let her outside. Having someone you love murdered changes you.

Kaia took one last sip of her hot chocolate and set the mug down, gathering her things. Homeward bound, it was. She popped her earbuds out, tucked them away in her pocket, and pulled her black scarf up over her ears to keep warm. It wasn't like New Mexico got too cold, but when you were up in the mountains, the winters could be nippy.

It was twilight now—Kaia's favorite time of the day. It was always quiet by then. The world was usually loud, but at twilight, it would shut up just enough for Kaia to get a little peace.

Living, for Kaia, was slow. She was homeschooled, rarely went out, and didn't like going to crowded areas. Her dad had asked her if other people made her nervous, but it wasn't anything like that. Kaia just felt disinterested. *But*, she thought, *the world is beautiful if you look at it closely.* Maybe she wasn't trying hard enough.

Kaia's pace slowed along the sidewalk. She'd have to cross the road up ahead but was in no rush. Her dad would have her head when she got back for staying out so late, but she didn't particularly care. She loved him for trying, but he'd changed after Kaia's mom died. He became distant like he didn't know what to do with Kaia or Cole now that he didn't have anyone to share the burden with. And it wasn't like she had been particularly close to him before. Kaia had always been her mom's daughter.

The moon was just starting to appear. Kaia leaned against one of the wooden fences that lined the road leading back to her house. The Neighborhood, Kaia's favorite and only coffee place, was only about a five-minute walk from home. Its proximity was the only reason why she was allowed there. Her dad would wonder why it had taken her so long to get back.

But the moon was beautiful. It was almost full, so close that she had to look closely to tell that it wasn't. An overwhelming sadness overcame Kaia. It was the anniversary, and Kaia was alone. She was still alone. For some reason, looking up at the moon was a reminder of how small she was. So, why was it that her loneliness felt so endless?

*You know, Kaia…*Her mom's words surfaced out of the blue. Kaia couldn't remember what her voice sounded like, though. It had been too long, and there were no videos or recordings to remind Kaia. It was terrifying how quickly things like that faded. She could remember the exact words, but not the voice.

Someone will come. One day, I won't be there to look after you. You'll have to be brave, baby, but someone will come. Keep an open mind and an open heart. I never want you to be lonely.

Kaia wiped away a tear before it could fall and squeezed her eyes shut. The afterimage of the moon hovered behind her eyelids. She was so young when her mom said that. As a child, she resisted the thought. Imagining life without her mother there to protect her seemed impossible. Now that it had become her reality, Kaia just didn't want to be alone. Her mother would be sad if she saw Kaia now.

When she opened her eyes, it was in shock. The most fantastic smell had hit her nose, forcing her to tilt her head up to catch it better. She inhaled deeply, letting it fill her up. It smelled like a weird mixture of wood smoke and fir trees. Kaia looked around, curious about its origin. She wasn't near any trees, so it wasn't that. But then it vanished almost as quickly as it had appeared.

An odd experience, without a doubt, but not bizarre enough to put her life on pause. She hugged herself, continuing on her way. Another shiver ran through her. This time, it was because a feeling had sprung up in the pit of her stomach—a strange nervousness. Her heart beat quickly the rest of the way home. When she finally got back and shut the door behind her, she leaned heavily against it and closed her eyes again.

She remembered that smell, especially how it had made her skin tingle. Her mom's words echoed in her head again. *If you do anything at all, Kaia, do it with all the passion you can muster. Don't settle for anything less.*

Kaia wondered if that was why she was alone; no matter what stranger she interacted with, even against her dad's wishes, she could never muster the energy for opening herself up to them. She wasn't sure why. Then her mom's words came once more.

You know, Kaia, someone will come.

"Kaia, what took you so long to get back here? I texted you fifteen minutes ago," her dad said, rounding the corner. He must have heard the door shut. He stared at her, adjusting his glasses on the bridge of his nose.

"Sorry," she said quietly. "I…got distracted. My head hurts a lot." Mostly the truth, but she wasn't about to mention how badly she hadn't wanted to come home. Her dad wouldn't have that, and she didn't need to make his job harder. The headache part was entirely accurate, though. A splitting headache had come out of nowhere.

"It's dangerous for you outside this late at night," he said, ushering her farther inside with a hand on her back. "And you're cold. Take a warm bath. We'll talk later."

Kaia smiled to herself. That sounded nice.

☾

Kaia lifted her hand, watching little waterfalls cascade off her skin as she did. She stared at her legs, which were so long that they pressed up against the far side of the tub. She sighed.

A knock came at the door. "Kaia, you've been in there for a century."

A helpful reminder from her little brother, Cole, who was about as impatient as a seventeen-year-old can get. "Give the rest of the world a turn."

She heard stomping footsteps fade as Cole left the door. Kaia sighed. She probably had around ten minutes before Cole would somehow manage to unlock the door and barge in. He did it before, and he'd do it again. The bath was helping, but her head was still pounding a bit. Her brother, on the other hand, wasn't helping at all.

Kaia looked out the window, high on the wall above the tub. The room was dark. Kaia didn't bother to turn the lights on before she climbed into the water. The moon was bright enough that she didn't need them. She liked the moonlight. Her skin looked pale and perfect underneath it. Her long, platinum blonde hair looked almost silver.

Kaia jerked upright, lifting her nose up to the air again. It was that smell from earlier, but this time, it was stronger, closer. Kaia gripped the edge of the tub. It was so cold under her pruned fingers.

For some reason, she was compelled to look out the window. So she did. She eased herself upright, standing so that she could peek over the window frame. The window looked down at their house's little backyard on the edge of the forest, right near a little canyon.

Kaia stared at the moon again for a moment, intimidated by the longing that sprung up whenever she inhaled. That scent, now reminding her of wood smoke, made Kaia think of better times—of pure happiness. It was sweet. So, so sweet.

And then something caught Kaia's eye. Something was shifting along the forest edge. Whatever it was, it was big and black, causing sticks to crack and branches to whip around as it brushed past. Kaia stared, squinting and leaning forward so that she could see it better.

If she'd been younger, she'd have been too afraid to look. But not now. Now, this mystery was intriguing. The tiny drop of fear in her veins only made it more exciting.

Kaia watched the massive shape move silently along the edge of the forest, stalking back and forth as if it were hesitant to venture farther. Kaia tilted her head to the side, entranced. It was elegant despite its size. Its every movement was calculated, deliberate.

A set of yellow eyes flashed up at her, and she froze. They bore into her, staring up at her from the shadows where the creature hid. Kaia was scared at first. She couldn't even move.

She began to shiver. *His* eyes didn't stray from her. Gradually, she realized that he was there for her. She could understand him so clearly. It was like she could hear what he was thinking, and her fear melted. He was, indeed, there for her. He thought she was beautiful, a silver goddess shining a light down on him from high above his head.

Kaia was his moon, and he didn't even know her name.

Then Kaia realized that she was still completely naked, staring at a shifty stranger who was lurking in the bushes. She quickly covered herself with a squeak and stashed herself away under the water, feeling it burn her cooled skin.

Bumps had sprung up on her arms, and she rubbed them vigorously until they faded. Kaia reached forward and pulled hard. The usual gurgling noise indicated that the tub was draining.

Kaia shakily stood again and wrapped herself in a crisp white towel, squeezing the excess water out of her hair. The smell of fir trees hadn't entirely faded from her nose when she went to stand in front of the foggy mirror.

She sighed. She could still feel him all around her. A part of her felt uneasy, but some irrational piece of her heart was whispering excitedly. She felt more alive than she had in a long time.

Kaia had heard in the past that she was lovely. She had skin so pale and creamy she seemed a sheltered princess. She was tall, thin, and delicate, with long, platinum hair that fell softly around her chest. Beyond pretty, her face carried echoes of her mother's exotic heritage, with dark almond eyes that stood out on her face and full lips that looked like they should always be spinning fantastic tales. Her slightly unusual features were one of the few things she'd gotten from her mom; she also inherited a habit of tilting her head to the side just right, which made her seem mysterious and clever.

But there is often a difference between what people say and how you feel. Just out of the bath, she could only imagine that she looked like a pathetic wet dog. Her face was a bit blotchy and red from the steaming water. There was a hauntingly empty look about her. The usual spark in her eyes was missing. She looked like the ghost of herself. Yes, she was beautiful, but in a bedraggled sort of manner; she had lost so much, and anyone looking at her now would be able to tell.

But Kaia remembered as tingles danced around her pale skin. That's not how he saw her.

In his eyes, she glowed. The wet tendrils of her hair, stuck to her shoulders and her shivering chest, looked like silver rivers gloriously falling between her breasts. Her pale, milky skin was like a canvas waiting for him to paint it with his dark colors. To him, she was the moon. To him, she was so agonizingly tempting, maybe even dangerously so. If he were to reach out and touch her with just the tips of his fingers, he doubted he'd be able to stop again.

She looked like hope.

Kaia hugged herself, letting that exquisite image fill her heart up. Because, at that moment, she wasn't alone. That was all that Kaia had ever wanted.

If you enjoyed this sample, look for
His Moon
on Amazon.

ACKNOWLEDGEMENTS

I want to acknowledge my family whom also encourage me to pursue my dreams. They stuck by my side through thick and thin.

AUTHOR'S NOTE

Thank you so much for reading *The Hunting Game*! I can't express how grateful I am for reading something that was once just a thought inside my head.

Please feel free to send me an email. Just know that my publisher filters these emails. Good news is always welcome.
leila_vy@awesomeauthors.org

I'd love to hear your thoughts on the book. Please leave a review on Amazon or Goodreads because I just love reading your comments and getting to know you!

Can't wait to hear from you!

Leila Vy

ABOUT THE AUTHOR

I have completed my associates degree in Computer Science and am currently working on a bachelor of Healthcare Business Management. I have worked in many business industries, but currently, I am employed in the healthcare industry. Aside from work, I enjoy traveling and exploring the different cultures. One of my favorite things to do on my free time is reading, writing books, and graphic designing. I came from an overly large-sized family, and so I enjoy big parties and social events.

www.ingramcontent.com/pod-product-compliance
Lightning Source LLC
Chambersburg PA
CBHW031507210626
46807CB00026B/2469